# Shandra Higheagle Mystery Series

*Double Duplicity*

*Tarnished Remains*

*Deadly Aim*

*Murderous Secrets*

# Double Duplicity

## A Shandra Higheagle Mystery

Paty Jager

Trish,
Enjoy Shandra's
journey~
Thanks for buying!
Paty

DOUBLE DUPLICITY
Copyright © 2015 Patricia Jager

Contact Information: info@windtreepress.com
Windtree Press
Beaverton, Oregon
Visit us at http://windtreepress.com

Cover Art by Christina Keerins
Photography by: Tim Norman Arts

Published in the United States of America
ISBN 9781940064925

## Acknowledgement

I would like to thank Tim Norman Arts (http://timnormanarts.com/) for the use of their gallery and people for the staging of the cover photo and to Tim Norman, my brother, for his insight into how bronze statues are made and assembled. His knowledge of the art world is what helped me conjure up my character, Shandra Higheagle.

Chapter One

The Bluetooth in Shandra Higheagle's Jeep rang, interrupting the memories and drumbeats swirling in her head. She shook the past couple days off and pushed the green phone icon on the radio screen.

"Shandra."

"Hi Shandra, this is Paula Doring. I know this is short notice, but I really would like to speak with you if you're coming down off your mountain today."

Shandra rolled her eyes. Of all the gallery owners in Huckleberry, Paula was her least favorite. The woman didn't understand artists and thought only of the dollar.

"I am off my mountain. I should be rolling into Huckleberry in about twenty minutes."

"Perfect. Could you swing by my gallery? I have a new acquisition, and I think a couple of your vases would look wonderful partnered with it. See you in twenty." Paula hung up.

"Great! One more thing to interfere with getting my vases to Ted and Naomi." Ted and Naomi Norton, owners of Dimensions Gallery, were expecting her to deliver more vases for the art event beginning tonight. They were her best supporters and showcased her vases in their gallery.

She only had one piece at Paula's gallery, aptly named after her, Doring Art Gallery. Paula was known to only take in artists she felt would propel her gallery to a status, rather than taking in artists that she liked. But she'd insisted on having at least one piece of Shandra's art so she could also say she had one thing from all the local artists.

As much as she didn't care for Paula, who was a backstabber, she did want her pieces seen and having more than one in the Doring Gallery for the upcoming art event that was the most publicized show in the Pacific Northwest was a good move on her part. Her latest gourd-shaped pieces were recently the focus of a story in the *Northwest Art Magazine*. The exposure had garnered her more sales and attention. While she liked traveling to shows, right now, her heart was at home with her animals and her clay.

The resort village of Huckleberry Mountain sat fifteen miles off Idaho I-90 at the base of the Bitterroot Mountains. Shandra turned onto Huckleberry Highway and soon slowed to turn right toward the town. Turning left would take her to the Ski Lodge. Art collectors who had gathered at the resort for the event would be dining at the Lodge's five-star restaurant tomorrow night after schmoozing over cocktails and appetizers with the local artists.

Shandra didn't care for the schmoozing, but the people who bought the high priced art sold in the galleries wanted to be on a first name basis with the artists who envisioned their pieces.

She obeyed the twenty miles per hour signs driving down Huckleberry Street. The speed felt like she was crawling after keeping the cruise on seventy most of the way from Nespelem and her grandmother's funeral. Driving fast hadn't dislodged the uneasy feeling her grandmother had requested she attend the seven drum ceremony for a reason. "But what reason?"

Shandra parked the Jeep at the curb across from the Doring Gallery. She caught a glimpse of her friend Naomi, jogging across the side street.

*Where could Naomi have been coming from*? "The bank, the bakery?" Shandra said out loud as she'd become accustom to talking to herself from hours spent alone with her animals as she crafted her art.

She stepped out of the Jeep, straightened her leopard print, tiered skirt, smoothed a hand over her denim shirt, and shifted the concho belt around so the dangling end was at her right hip. She slung the fringed leather bag over her shoulder and headed across the street, dodging the slow moving traffic. Her cowboy boot heels echoed when she stepped onto the tiled entryway of Doring Gallery. The buzz of her entry died in the stillness.

"Paula? Paula, it's Shandra." She continued through the middle of the partitions spattered with various sizes of paintings and prints and pedestals honoring handcrafted masterpieces.

"Paula?" It wasn't like Paula to leave the gallery unmanned, or as the case may be unwomanned. If Paula wasn't here, where was Juan, her assistant? A shiver slithered up Shandra's back as she moved deeper into the building.

A display of Native American art caught her attention. Vibrant photos of twenty-first century ceremonial dancers covered one partition while paintings of historical depictions covered the other. The crease in the partition at the apex of the V reminded her of the world she'd just come from at the reservation. Her grandmother's funeral had been half modern and half the old ways. It had been the ceremony of the old ways that lightened her sad heart.

An abstract horse and rider stood four feet tall in the middle of the V-shaped display while two four-foot tall warriors stood guard on either side. One held a bow, the other a spear. The convergence of the abstract modern piece and the steadfast, solid bronze statues that depicted the way Native Americans are seen in history mirrored her life.

Shandra dismissed the pondering about her roots and pulled her gaze from the bronze six-pack on the warrior with the spear and headed toward the office. She had to give Paula credit; the gallery owner knew how to display art to its fullest advantage.

"Paula?" A light shone around the edges of the partially open office door. Shandra pushed the door open. "Why aren't you answer—"

Paula's arms hung splayed away from her body that was cradled in her leather office chair. A large red patch spread across her body and lifeless eyes stared up at the ceiling.

Shandra backed out of the room. She couldn't swallow for the lump of fear and vileness she'd just witnessed.

"Think… Call the police." She punched in 9 as sirens shrieked and grew louder. "Maybe they're coming here." *They had to be coming here. This town is too small for there to be two incidents where the cops are needed at the same time.*

She put her phone in her bag and strode toward the front of the building.

The door buzzed. A young officer she'd never seen before burst into the building with his gun held in front of him.

"Stop! Put your hands in the air!" he shouted.

Shandra squeaked and raised her arms.

"Did you call the cops?"

"No. I—"

He advanced on her so fast she didn't know what was happening until he wrenched her arm behind her back.

"What are you doing?" she asked as pain twinged up her arm.

"I'm detaining you until I can search the premises." He cuffed her and started to haul her to the door.

"Oh, no, you don't. I'm not going into a squad car and looking like a criminal when I'm not. I just arrived and found Paula in the office. I was starting to call nine-one-one when I heard the sirens." Shandra dug in her boot heels. There was no way she'd have the whole town see her sitting in a cop car. She'd done nothing wrong.

"Who's Paula?" He tugged on her, but she refused to be humiliated for nothing.

"The owner of the gallery. She's in her chair in the office. Dead." That stopped the zealous officer.

"We received a phone call of suspicious activity." He changed course, pushing her ahead of him to the back of the building and the office.

Shandra complied. She'd rather stand by the office door while he did his thing than be seen in a cop car.

At the office, Blane, his name tag said, stood her next to the door. "Don't move. You're still a suspect."

She nodded. She'd stay here all day if she didn't have to look at Paula again.

He entered the office. "Holy shit."

Shandra couldn't have said it better. She heard him moving around before he came back out. He pushed the button on the radio receiver clipped to his shoulder.

"Dispatch, this is Blane. We've got a homicide over at Doring Gallery on Huckleberry Street. I have a suspect in custody."

"Now wait a minute—"

He silenced her with a swipe of his hand through the air.

"Don't let anyone else enter and don't leave the premises until a detective gets there." The excitement in the dispatcher's voice reminded Shandra this resort town rarely had excitement of this magnitude.

This was big news for Huckleberry. Sad news, but big news. She didn't like to think someone from their small town could be a murderer. She knew most of the locals.

She'd purchased the old Whitmire ranch thirty miles north of town two years ago. That was three years after she'd graduated from college and received enough of an inheritance from her maternal grandmother to try her hand at pottery. Her search for a place had taken a while. One of the reasons being she needed land with a certain type of clay soil. She found it on the ranch. The clay had become her signature in her pottery.

Officer Blane yanked on her arm. "I'm gonna sit you in the extra chair in the office."

"Oh no, you're not. You bring that chair out here. I'm not sitting in there and staring at Paula. The one glimpse I had is enough to haunt me." She glared at the man, thankful he was only a few years past puberty and she stood several inches taller than the officer, making it easier to intimidate him.

He ducked into the room, pulled the extra chair out, and Shandra gladly sat down. For all the bravado she showed the officer, her knees were knocking together. She was his only suspect for the killing. She was innocent. But growing up, she'd witnessed more than one Native American person be railroaded. It was the reason her mother and stepfather forbid her to talk about her father's family. They felt she would be persecuted. The small ranch community in Montana where they lived was tolerant of very little.

Chapter Two

Detective Ryan Greer slowly unfolded from the unmarked Tahoe he used as a Weippe County detective. He'd moved back to northern Idaho to escape the crazies he'd battled while a detective with the Chicago Police Department. He hadn't been back two months and he received a call from the Weippe sheriff asking him to take this job. The highbrow resort town of Huckleberry had been way out of his league growing up, but now, as a county detective, it was part of his jurisdiction.

Dispatch said they had the killer in custody. He'd have to high-five the local P.D. for acting so quickly and apprehending the culprit. He'd only received the call an hour ago. Having a suspect in custody made his job easier. He slung a backpack with his forensic kit over one shoulder and walked up to the entrance.

He raised the yellow crime scene tape and ducked

under to enter the building. A buzzer announced his entry along with the echo of his boot heels on the tiles as he walked into the art gallery.

"Hello?" He studied his notebook. "Officer Blane?"

"Back here!"

Ryan walked to the back of the building. His gaze landed on the woman with long dark hair who sat as ridged as his grandmother's straight-backed dining chair. This couldn't be the murderer, could it? As the thought emerged in his mind, her head swiveled slowly toward him. He was struck first by the light golden color of her eyes and second by the raised chin and defiance etched on her face.

A pimply-faced kid dressed in the local P.D.s uniform stepped out of the shadow of an open door.

"Officer Blane," the kid said, sticking out his hand.

Not taking his eyes off the woman seated in the chair, Ryan gripped the upstart's hand a bit firmly. "Detective Ryan Greer."

He directed his first question to the woman. "Who are you?"

"Shandra Higheagle." Her voice was husky and not at all what he'd expected.

He turned to Blane. "Why is she handcuffed?" He placed a hand under Ms. Higheagle's elbow and helped her stand.

"I found her in here when I responded to the suspicious activity call." Blane pulled out his notebook.

Ryan dipped his finger into his jean pocket and pulled out a handcuff key.

"Hey! She's my suspect," Blane said, stepping forward.

Ryan stopped him by raising the hand with the key. "What are you doing here?" he asked Ms. Higheagle.

"I didn't kill Paula. She called me to meet her here. I arrived and found her…" The woman nodded toward the open door.

"What did you do after you found her?" Ryan kept his gaze steady on the woman. It wasn't a hardship to study her high cheekbones and wide expressive golden eyes.

"I backed out of the room and started to dial nine-one-one when I heard sirens coming, so I walked to the front of the building and officer Blane came in like a cop on some TV show, all guns first and not listening to my side of the circumstances."

Ryan shoved the key into the cuffs and released the lock. When the cuffs were removed from Ms. Higheagle, she rubbed her wrists and glared at Blane. Ryan studied her hands and clothing. He didn't see any blood or evidence of a weapon. He'd search her more closely once he determined the manner of death.

"Would you remain here with officer Blane while I take a look at the victim? I'll have more questions for you once I've had a look around."

She nodded and sat back down on the chair.

His gut told him she wasn't a murderer, but he had to see the cause of death to be able to rule her out. It didn't sound like she'd had enough time to stash a weapon or clean up before Blane arrived.

He slipped his pack off his shoulder and extracted booties and latex gloves from the outside pockets before swinging it back onto his shoulder. He pulled the booties over his cowboy boots and wrestled his hands into the latex gloves.

The metallic tang of blood assaulted his nostrils as he stepped into the room. The scent stopped his feet and sent his mind spinning back in time to the gang fight he'd walked into in Chicago. There were many who left the alley in body bags. The scent of blood had permeated the whole alley where the two gangs had used every weapon they could get their hands on to annihilate the other.

His month long hospital stay, six months of grueling rehab, and then facing the leaders of the gangs as he testified at their trials was one horrendous bad dream. As soon as his part in the trials was over, his resignation hit the commander's desk and he came home.

Ryan shook his head clearing it of the past and stared at the woman sprawled in the chair, staring at the ceiling. His gaze immediately landed on the large dark spot covering her chest. From lack of blood on the floor, if it was a bullet, it didn't exit the back. Making it a small caliber and less likely anyone heard the shot. He peered closer. The large amount of blood and ripped clothing around the wound dismissed his thoughts of it being a bullet that caused the wound.

He slid a hand into the outside pocket of the backpack and pulled out his digital camera. The click of photos, one by one capturing the scene from all angles, triggered his detective mode. He forgot all else, moving in a circle, closing in on the body. Standing over the body, he looked straight down at her chest. The torn clothing at the entry sight and the gaping hole with pink foam…*this wasn't caused by a clean stab of a knife, it was viciously twisted to cause maximum damage*.

The click of the camera continued as he took

photos from every possible angle of the wound and the body. Halfway through his inspection and photos, he spotted drops of blood on the desk. One on a paper, another on what looked like an abstract of a… He crouched down eye level. It was two bodies entwined in the act of sex.

Ryan shook his head. Where had that come from? Staring at the object from a standing position it appeared to be a stack of sticks. Shoving the impression of the art piece from his mind, he concentrated on finding more drops.

One, on the floor headed to a door.

A push on the unlatched door revealed a small restroom. He crossed to the sink, pulled out the luminol spray and sprayed the rim of the drain for blood. Shining his black light flashlight on the drain, he snapped a photo of the luminesce image circling the drain. The killer had washed the weapon or their hands or both before leaving.

He placed everything back into his bag, except for the luminol. It was time to talk to the one witness they had and test her hands for traces of blood.

Chapter Three

Shandra fidgeted on the hard chair. She pulled out her cell phone and checked the time. 3:45. She had a forty-five minute drive to her place, pack seven vases, and drive back down here to deliver them to Ted and Naomi before they closed the gallery at six to open for the special twilight showing tonight from nine to midnight. She didn't want to drag them to the gallery during their three hours to get dinner and dress for the special show. They'd had a rough year with business and personal turmoil.

The tall detective came out of Paula's office. He carried a spray bottle and stopped in front of her chair.

"Ms. Higheagle, would you please hold out your hands?" He said it as a request but his tone sounded like a demand.

She had nothing to hide and held her hands out palm up. He sprayed the cold liquid on her hands. It stung a cut she had from her carving utensil. She winced and he frowned.

"Sorry to do that, but I had to rule you out as a suspect. Whoever killed the victim—"

"Paula Doring," Shandra said. It made the whole episode seem less vile by calling the dead woman by her name and not "victim."

He nodded and wrote the name in a small notebook he'd pulled from a pocket on his backpack. "Whoever killed Ms. Doring would have blood residue on their hands. She was killed at close proximity." His dark brown eyes scanned her hands before he turned his attention to Officer Blane.

"Get the local M.E. over to substantiate the death and call the forensic lab in Coeur d'Alene to let them know I'm bringing them a body." Detective Greer waited for the officer to walk to the front of the gallery talking on his radio.

"Ms. Higheagle, please tell me exactly what you saw and did when you arrived."

"Call me Shandra if you don't mind. Ms. Higheagle was my grandmother." She'd only started using her father's last name after high school. Before that she'd gone as Shandra Malcolm, using her stepfather's last name even though he never legally adopted her. Ella, her paternal grandmother, made a fuss any time Shandra's mother suggested her stepfather might adopt her. Ella never said anything outright, but her actions showed she didn't care for Shandra's stepfather.

"Shandra, you said earlier Ms. Doring called you. Why?"

"There is a large art event happening this weekend

in Huckleberry." She crossed her arms. "In fact, it starts tonight at nine. I should be home packing pieces to bring to the Dimensions Gallery across the street." She tipped her head toward the side street. Her mind flashed to the sight of Naomi jogging across that same street as she'd parked the Jeep.

"What are you thinking? Did you see someone?" The detective jumped on her momentary flash like a ravenous dog on a bowl of kibble.

"No. I-I had an idea for a new piece." She wasn't going to give up her good friend until she had a chance to find out why Naomi was hurrying from this side of the street. "Anyway, Paula called me to come by and discuss placing a few of my vases in her gallery for this weekend. She said she had some new Native American pieces come in and wanted to display my latest gourd vases with them."

"Was it normal for her to call you?"

His intense gaze made her feel like she was on trial even though he'd pretty much admitted he believed her innocent. That irked. She didn't lie, but could skirt the truth a fraction until the right moment to tell the truth presented itself.

"You had to know Paula. She liked to make you feel inferior, and she did it best face to face." *Oh, that wasn't good.* Her irritation at him made her sound like a suspect.

His left dark eyebrow rose. "That's not a very friendly image of the woman."

Shandra stared him straight in the eye. "You'll find she had few friends. I wouldn't say she had enemies, but anyone who has ever dealt with Paula didn't come out of it a friend." Several stanzas of a jazz classic

21

boogied in her purse. She pulled the phone out and looked at the number.

Ted.

"Can I answer this? It's the gallery that's waiting for my vases."

Detective Greer nodded once.

She pushed the button and answered. "Hi, Ted."

"Shandra, I saw your Jeep parked across the street for a couple hours. Why haven't you brought the vases in?" Ted's frazzled tone made her wish she hadn't taken the call from Paula earlier.

"I'm actually at Paula's gallery—"

The detective cleared his throat and shook his head.

She held the phone against her thigh. "It's not like he can't see the crime scene tape, you know."

"Just tell him you'll be detained for a little while longer."

"How long? It's a forty-five minute drive to my ranch." She held up her fingers. "Figure one hour there, so I don't speed—" she tossed him an ingratiating smile—"half an hour to pack the vases unless I call Lil and have her get them packed…" That was a thought. Her housekeeper/groundskeeper knew the pieces she wanted to have at the show.

"Ask him to wait for you." Greer motioned with his hand to speed up the conversation.

"Ted, I'm sorry. I've been detained. But I promise I won't be there any later than six-thirty. I have to go." She pushed the end button to Ted's stammering. She hated to be so short with such a good friend, but she had no choice at the moment. She'd call him back on the drive home.

"I'm sorry this is bad timing for you, but you're the

only witness I have so far. I need your statement before I escort the body to the coroner." He leaned against the door jamb.

"Paula called when I was about twenty minutes from here."

"What time was that?"

"About one-thirty or one-forty. I'm not sure. I didn't really pay much attention." She hadn't even looked at the time when she answered the call; she just knew the road well enough to know how long it would take.

"Where were you coming from?" His head remained bent as he scribbled in his notebook.

"My grandmother's funeral in Nespelem, Washington."

His face tipped up, and his eyes softened. "I'm sorry for your loss."

"Thank you." She stared into his dark eyes. He'd suffered a similar loss. It was in the look and the softening of his expression.

He dropped his gaze to the notepad in his hand. "So you arrived here at two or a little after?"

She shrugged. "I guess so. I didn't look at the time, just parked, crossed the street, and walked in the door. I thought it odd Paula didn't meet me since she had requested my visit. I called out, didn't hear anything, and worked my way through the gallery back here to the office. I saw the light on and called out again." She squeezed her eyes shut to push the sight of Paula from her mind. "She didn't answer, so I pushed the door open, and saw her."

"Did you enter the room?"

Shandra thought back. "No. I backed out and

pulled my phone out of my purse to call nine-one-one. I punched in the nine and heard the sirens. This town rarely has anything happen that warrants a siren. I figured someone already called this in and headed to the front of the gallery. That's when Roscoe P. Coltrane jumped through the doorway with his gun pointed at me and handcuffed me without getting my side of the story."

"So you're a Dukes of Hazard fan." Detective Greer smiled at her. "I'm thinking it was his first call of this nature since putting on the suit. Don't hold his overachieving attitude against him." The levity of the moment passed when he glanced up and speared her with a dark brown gaze. "Did you see anyone else in the vicinity when you arrived?"

A flash of Naomi crossing the street caused her to drop her gaze. She couldn't implicate her friend without questioning her first. "I didn't see anything out of the ordinary."

Detective Greer took a step closer to her. She'd have to tilt her head back to look him in the eye. She preferred to stare at the black snaps of his western cut shirt.

"I asked if you saw anyone in the vicinity. Who did you see on this block or the next?"

His calm tone and deep voice, only made her feel worse about withholding information.

"There were some tourists, I guess, on the sidewalks. Anyway, they weren't people I know."

He placed a finger under her chin, raising her face to look up at him. "I don't know who you're covering for, but I'll find out."

Looking into his confident dark eyes, she didn't

doubt he would, but she'd talk with Naomi before he figured it out.

Chapter Four

Ryan watched the flimsy leopard print skirt swish as Shandra Higheagle sashayed out the front door of the gallery, her boot heels clicking on the tile. The woman was hiding something. She'd stared him straight in the eye and been defiant until he asked if she saw anyone. Then she'd evaded his question and looked everywhere but at him.

He pivoted back to the office and the dead body. There wasn't anything more the body would tell him until forensics discovered the weapon that made the wound. He strode to the desk and thumbed through her day planner. She'd had lots of appointments today. It would help if someone could tell him who the people listed in the book were; clients, artists, or what. He should have asked Shandra if the woman ran the gallery by herself.

Two contracts for consignment of art pieces signed

today sat in a wire box labeled to file. He looked down and noticed a drawer pulled out an inch. Did someone pull it out, take something, and then not get it shoved back in? He dusted the handle and front of the drawer for fingerprints and came up with several from the flat front surface.

Hooking his fingers through the handle on the drawer, he tugged. A cash box, ledger, and several files rested in the drawer.

Could this have been a robbery gone wrong? The cash box was average sized and not locked. The lid lifted easily, revealing several hundred dollars and a handful of checks. If this had been a robbery, the cash would be gone. He closed the box and pulled out the ledger.

Names graced the left column in the book and rows of numbers lined the pages. Some were dates, some dollar amounts. Red, blue, and black dollar amounts. He'd never liked accounting. He placed the ledger on the desk along with the cash box.

The files held artist brochures. The bright red words "GET" and "NO" were sprawled across each sculpture or painting on the brochures. Either these were pieces already in the gallery or ones she planned to acquire. He matched several of the names on the brochures to the names in the ledger. In doing so, he noticed large sums of money being logged into the ledger at the beginning of each month but no notation as to where the money came from.

Ryan placed the ledger and the files in his backpack. He'd have time to go through them thoroughly after the body was examined by the coroner and he spent the night in Coeur d'Alene. The trip wouldn't be a bust. He could crash at his sister's place and not add to the county's expenses.

Voices and muffled footsteps along with the whir of rubber wheels on tile grew near. The medical examiner and the local funeral home had arrived. Now he'd get more answers about any employees and the woman.

A man, a few years younger than Ryan's thirty-two years, walked toward the office as Ryan stepped out to greet the doctor who worked as the county coroner. Dr. Maynard Porter was not a typical coroner or rural doctor for that matter. He was of slender build, so blond he appeared almost albino, and dressed like a model from some fancy men's magazine. Ryan had only met the man once before, when a body had been found by hunters. He'd bet the ink hadn't dried on Dr. Porter's medical license yet.

"Dr. Porter," Ryan extended his still-gloved hand.

The doctor shook hands and nodded toward the open doorway. "Tell me it isn't the owner of the gallery."

Ryan perked up. The doctor knew his victim. "Wish I could. It's Paula Doring, and it's not a pretty sight."

Porter shook his head. "This is going to slow up my purchase of a painting I'd planned to buy this weekend." With no remorse for the woman, he sauntered into the office.

Ryan motioned for the funeral home attendant to wait with the gurney and hurried in behind the doctor.

"Did you know the victim well?" Ryan pulled out his pencil and notepad.

"Only well enough to know she drove a hard

bargain and wasn't well liked. But she was respected by both the patrons and the artists." Dr. Porter picked up her arm to feel the pulse. His white eyebrows rose. "She's fresh."

"From my calculations she was killed three hours ago." He jotted down the doctor's reaction to the time. "Does she run the gallery alone?"

Dr. Porter closed the victim's eyelids. "She has a part time employee. Juan something. I've only talked with him once. Nice enough guy but not really personable. By his attitude, I'd say he was more an artist who worked here to supplement his income."

"How's that?" The doctor seemed well educated on the local scene.

Porter looked up from writing on a paper on a clipboard. "If you go to one of the art events here you'll see what I mean. The owners and employees of the galleries are talkative, smiling, wanting to draw you into their little world and buy from them. Most artists are all about the art and while they are required to be at the events, they stand to the edges, talking with other artists or staring at their own work. They don't mingle, don't do idle chit-chat." Porter clicked his pen closed. "Juan is hard to talk to, moody, and only had eyes for Paula. He'd watch her moving around in here and at events like she was his work of art." The doctor nodded to the body. "She's all yours. Hope you find the person responsible."

"Me too." Ryan closed his notepad. The doctor's information gave him more to examine about the woman and her employee.

Dr. Porter picked up his leather bag and exited the office. Ryan poked his head out. "Come get the body."

He stepped back as a large man, as opposite on the color spectrum from the doctor as he could get, entered the room.

"Maxwell Treat, at your service," said the man, smiling and showing off a mouthful of large white teeth.

"Detective Ryan Greer."

The man's large hand gripped firm and decisive. "Pleased to meet you. I heard there's a body needs hauled to Coeur d'Alene."

Ryan stepped aside, revealing the victim.

"Well now, I expected her to be stabbed in the back not the front." Treat pulled the gurney into the room.

"You know the victim?" Ryan dipped into his pocket for the pencil and pad.

"She turned down Naomi's sister and gave the assistant job to some Hispanic that can barely speak English." Treat unzipped the body bag, pulled on latex gloves, and none-to-gently shoved the body in the bag.

"Naomi's sister have a name?"

Treat turned large dark brown eyes on him. "Joyce Carter. If you plan to talk with her you'll need to hold a séance."

His pencil stopped. "What happened?"

"How long you been living in these parts?"

The disgust in the man's voice and visible anger on his face led Ryan to believe the death wasn't from natural causes. "Three months give or take a couple weeks."

"Last year, Joyce was getting her life back together after being hooked on drugs and having her boyfriend locked up for distributing. Naomi and Ted took her in when she came out of rehab. Things were looking good until she applied for a job with Paula and the woman dug up all Joyce's back history and spread it around town until no one would hire Joyce and the guy she'd been dating dumped her." Treat shook his head slowly. "I tried to get her on at the funeral home but it barely keeps my family in food and a roof.

"Two months after Paula turned her down and spread the rumors, Joyce was found in an alley. She'd overdosed." Treat glared into Ryan's eyes. "I ain't never believed she'd slip back into drugs. When we became friends, she told me it was her boyfriend who forced her to take drugs. She never wanted to."

"Is he still in jail?"

Treat nodded. "Yes, sir. I made Chief Sandberg check on that first thing after she was found."

"Is Naomi's last name Carter, too?"

Treat smiled and shook his head. "No. It's Norton. She and Ted own the gallery across the street."

Ryan added Naomi Norton to his list as Treat rolled the gurney out of the building. Ted and Naomi Norton own the gallery across the street. Ms. Higheagle had talked to a Ted about her vases. Ryan had a hunch he'd found what Ms. Higheagle was reluctant to reveal.

He'd follow the body to the State Examiner's office, gather what information he could, then spend the night at his sister's and get back here first thing in the morning. He had several suspects to interview and an art event to attend.

Chapter Five

Shandra called Lil the minute she was headed out of town, instructing her to get the seven vases ready to transport. She was halfway between her ranch and town when she returned Ted's call.

"What is going on?" he asked, without a greeting.

"Paula called me as I was coming into town and asked me to meet with her at the gallery. I arrived and found her dead."

The intake of breath on the other line was an uncharacteristic show of emotion from Ted. He was the cool, never flustered guy who settled those around him. "What do you mean found her dead? Was it like a heart attack or something?"

"No. She was murdered. Someone stabbed or shot her in the chest." Shandra scrunched her eyes closed a second to try and shove the sight from her mind. The sound of her tires crunching on gravel shot her eyelids up, and she whipped the Jeep back onto the pavement.

"Why would someone do that? She was hard to deal with but to kill her..." Ted's voice became muffled. "Naomi wants to know when you'll be delivering the vases."

"I'm headed home now. Lil is getting them boxed up. I'll load right up, turn around, and come back down the mountain." Her stomach growled. She'd skipped lunch and it looked like dinner was going to be late.

"So an hour and a half? We'll have pizza at the gallery when you arrive."

Gratitude washed over her, warming a part of her that had chilled the minute she saw Paula's still body. "Thanks, Ted. You two are wonderful friends."

She pushed the Bluetooth button and turned off the paved county road. The entrance to her ranch looked like any other forest service road, but two miles up a rough dirt track a beautiful meadow appeared. In the middle of the meadow sat her house, barn, and art studio. Her heart sung with happiness every time she cleared the pine trees and spotted the buildings. The first time she drove up the road she'd felt welcomed. Walking the mountainside, she'd found the type of clay needed for her vases. A sense of homecoming had washed over her, and she'd clung to her dog, Sheba's, fur and cried with happiness.

Lil stood by the studio door, one hand holding Sheba's collar and the other stroking Lewis, the cat, looped around her neck like an orange fur stole. The woman was hard to miss. Lil liked purple and wore it whether the clothing fit or not, using baling twine or any other string she could find to hold up pants or tie up the sleeves like old fashioned garters. Her gray hair sprang out from under her ball cap at odd lengths. Lil had come with the ranch just like the stray cat draped over her shoulders. The woman didn't talk much, but Shandra had learned Lil grew up on the ranch with her grandparents. The ranch had sold before their deaths, and Lil refused to move. The realtor said the sheriff had removed Lil several times and the woman always returned. When Shandra heard the woman's obsession with the ranch and saw how capable she was with animals and keeping things tidy, she hired her.

They made a good pair. Lil cleaned the house and the studio and handled most of the outside chores. She tended the horses and Sheba when Shandra went to art shows or taught classes at colleges.

The moment the Jeep motor died, Sheba broke from Lil's hold and ran to the vehicle, placing her large paws on the window and licking the glass. Shandra laughed and slowly shoved the door open after the dog dropped to her four legs.

"I was only gone three days, girl." She roughed up Sheba's black, floppy, furry ears and kissed her wide forehead. No one, not even the vet, could determine what breeds made up her canine friend, but everyone agreed she was adorable if not a bit on the slobbery side.

"To her way of thinking you were gone two months." Lil opened the door to the studio. Seven boxes stood on the prep table.

"Thank you for boxing up the vases, Lil. I was detained at the Doring Gallery. Paula called me to come by, and I found her dead."

Lil stopped Shandra's arm as she reached out to pick up the first box.

"How'd she die?"

"Either a gun shot or a stab wound." Shandra peered into the other woman's eyes. "You know anything I should?"

Lil shrugged and picked up a box, carrying it out to the Jeep. Shandra followed, placing her box next to the other one in the back. Lil stopped, stroked the cat still draped around her neck, and stared into the trees.

"Saw Paula and a man arguing behind the Quick Mart yesterday." Her gaze slipped from the trees and peered into Shandra's eyes. "His face was red and his hands shook."

"Could you hear what they were saying? Did you know the man?" Shandra felt a bit of the tension she'd been harboring ease from her muscles. If she could give the detective someone to investigate besides Naomi or herself, this weekend would go a lot smoother for both of them.

Lil shook her head. "But they knew each other. They hugged when they first met, then they started arguing." She walked back into the studio and picked up another box.

Shandra mulled this information over as they loaded the boxes. Sheba looked up at her with sad eyes. Shandra laughed and opened a back car door. "Okay, you can ride shotgun as long as you don't lick the window."

Sheba leaped into the back seat of the four door vehicle, and Shandra moved to the driver's door. Knowing Lil went to bed early, she said, "Please, leave the porch light on and one in the kitchen. I'll have to stay and visit with prospective buyers."

Lil nodded and locked the studio door.

Driving down the mountain with Sheba panting and rocking the Jeep as she shifted in the back seat, Shandra didn't feel as alone as she had on the drive from her grandmother's funeral. Whenever she was with animals, whether it was her dog or her horses, she felt she was with family. More so than she ever did living with her mother and stepfather. That was why she and Lil got along so well. The woman understood animals and treated them like family. Whatever happened in the woman's past, she'd suppressed it and now infused all her emotions onto the animals around her.

Driving past Doring Gallery, a chill chased down Shandra's back. She glanced at the entrance. The yellow crime scene tape was pulled taut across the door. Beyond the door, deeper into the gallery, she thought she saw a flash of light. Did the police turn off the light in the office? "Probably not." That had to be what she saw.

She turned down the side street and into the alley behind Dimensions Gallery. Naomi's cherry red Mustang convertible was parked in its usual spot on the side opposite the garbage dumpster. Shandra parked with the backend of her Jeep in line with the back loading door.

"Stay," she told Sheba, rolling the windows all down halfway and stepped out of her vehicle. She opened the backend and picked up a box. The back door clicked and Ted stepped out.

"I thought that was you turning the corner." He grabbed a box and followed her into the building.

"I hurried back. Is Naomi here?" She wanted to ask her friend about earlier in the day before they all sat down and visited over pizza.

"She just walked down to Rigatori's for the pizza." Ted headed back out the door for another box.

Shandra followed and fifteen minutes later the boxes were out of the Jeep and the vases out of the boxes and sitting on a bench in the back room.

Ted leaned close to one of them inspecting the leather and feather enhancements she'd added to the mouth of the gourd-shaped piece.

"I think these are some of your best work yet."

The awe in his voice brought a lump to her throat. From her first attempt at forming clay in a grade school art class, she'd been infatuated with molding the earth into shapes that could be useful and decorative. But she'd never believed she could make a living selling the objects she'd crafted.

"I think I've had some divine intervention on these pieces."

Ted turned from his inspection and peered at her. "How so?"

"I made all of these after Ella, my grandmother, became sick. I've been seeing the shapes in my dreams and when I start a project before I'm aware, the shape I intended is gone and these gourd shapes appear."

"If the people who browsed through here this afternoon are any indication, this shape is appealing to pottery collectors."

The back door opened. Pepperoni, tomato, and yeasty scents entered the back room before a pizza box and Naomi appeared.

A big smile covered Naomi's face, but the affection that usually softened the lines around her eyes wasn't there. The warmth had just started appearing in her smiles the last few weeks. Her sister's death had robbed her of her usual bubbly self.

Ted took the pizza box from his wife. "I'll clear a spot here on the set up table if you two want to gather drinks and plates."

Shandra took that cue to herd Naomi into the office. She shut the door and faced her friend.

"What were you doing about two this afternoon?"

Naomi's eyes widened before she looked away. "I was here, in the back, uncrating paintings from Geoffrey."

"No, you weren't. I saw you crossing the street between here and Paula's gallery. Then I walked into her gallery and found her dead."

Her friend began to tremble. Shandra stepped forward, pulling her into a hug. "I didn't tell the detective I saw you because I know in my heart you didn't kill her, but I need to hear you say it."

Naomi shook her head. "I didn't kill her. But I was in the gallery." Her head dropped, and she covered her face with her hands.

"What did you see?" A shiver spiraled up Shandra's spine. If her friend saw the killer what would keep him from killing again to hide his deed?

"No...I didn't see anyone. I saw photos of Joyce. They were...She was..." Naomi collapsed in her arms. "My baby sister posed for photos." She hiccupped as she talked and cried. "You could see she was high by the brightness in her eyes..."

"Where did you see these photos?" Shandra held Naomi away from her.

Ted opened the door. He spotted Naomi and crossed the small room in two strides, wrapping his arms around her. "What have you done?"

His accusing glare stung nearly as brutal as the wasp that stung Shandra on her eighth birthday.

"I asked her why I saw her coming from Paula's minutes before discovering a dead body." They might be her friends, but they all had a lot to lose if any of them were implicated in Paula's death.

Ted rubbed a hand up and down his wife's back. "Is this true? Were you at Paula's this afternoon?"

Naomi nodded, wiping her cheeks on her husband's shirt, making a streak of darker blue.

"Why?" Ted's voice was barely restrained as his Adam's apple bobbed nervously.

Shandra held her breath. What could Naomi have hoped to prove by confronting the woman?

"I found a wadded up note from Paula in Joyce's things I was finally washing to take to the thrift store. It mentioned information Paula had. I knew Paula went to lunch from one to two every day and closed up the gallery." She sniffed and wiped at her nose with a tissue.

"How did you get in?" Ted asked, watching his wife.

"I paid Juan to make me a copy of the key to the back door—"

Shandra's heart thumped in her chest. "That will lead the police right to you."

Ted's eyes held the same fear that banged around inside Shandra.

"Honey, I don't…" Ted shoved his hands in his pockets and backed away from Naomi.

The hurt in her eyes was more than Shandra could take. She wrapped her arms around her friend. "Let's forget how you got in for the moment. What did you find or see?"

"I went straight to her office and went through her desk drawers. She had a whole file on Joyce. Photos, arrest records. Her life was even worse than she told us." Naomi's gaze sought her husband's. "The photos were so awful, I just stood there staring, unbelieving my little sister could be the person in the photos. Then I heard the front door buzz and realized Paula must be coming back. I grabbed the file and hurried out the back door." She pushed out of Shandra's embrace and walked up to Ted. "I ran two blocks down the alley and shoved the file into the dumpster behind the donut shop. When I turned from the dumpster, the back door of Paula's gallery was closing. I bought donuts and used the alley to return to the gallery."

"That must have been the killer you saw entering through the back door. Did you lock it when you went out?" Shandra watched her friend concentrate.

Naomi shook her head. "No. I just ran out thinking it would lock automatically."

"He had to have been watching and waiting for you to leave." Dread lodged in Shandra's chest. "The killer used your entering the gallery as his cover to kill Paula."

Shandra believed her friend, but she doubted Detective Greer would believe Naomi's story.

Chapter Six

Ryan sat at his sister's kitchen table drinking coffee and wishing he'd stayed up gossiping about their siblings rather than trying to decipher Paula Doring's ledger.

"You look like someone who spent the night on the town and came home alone." Bridget winked and sat down at the table, placing her youngest, Wally, on her lap.

"I spent the night staring at the victim's ledger. There were large payments made to the gallery each month, but I can't figure out where they were coming from."

"Blackmail?"

"That's what it looks like. The name that follows it doesn't match up to anything or one on any of the other information I brought with me." He sipped the coffee and really looked at his sister over the top of the cup.

She'd been unusually chipper when he'd arrived at her doorstep after midnight. He'd waited at the coroner's office until they'd determined the murder weapon wasn't a clean knife wound, which he'd known. The coroner also determined it wasn't razor sharp and had caused as much bruising as slicing.

"So, what's got your eyes bouncing and your lips in a smug smile?" He took another sip of coffee and retrieved his phone from Wally's sticky, pudgy hands.

"Conor is getting married." Her grin spread, and she wiggled in her chair.

"Tell me who the poor girl is. You're about to wiggle that chair into pieces." His older brother had been dodging matrimony for years. With two sisters and a mother who believed the oldest should be married, he'd had more girls and women shoved at him than a soon-to-be groom at a strip club.

"Lissa Chambers."

He stilled the cup at his lips only long enough to register the narrowing of his sister's eyes.

"You said you were over her."

Bridget's sympathetic tone but grilling gaze didn't do anything for the jab of pain behind his eyes. It was just the late night and staring at the damn ledger for hours. Not that his older brother was marrying the girl he'd set his heart on marrying in seventh grade. That was until she'd dumped him to pursue a career in modeling. He'd joined the military, did his stint, and returned to learn she was no longer pursuing modeling, but wasn't in the least interested in carrying on a courtship with a policeman.

"I am over her, just didn't expect my big brother to marry her. The last time I saw her she was so cold and snooty I expected a blizzard to blow in. Wouldn't have thought a Greer was good enough for her." That was the vibe she'd given him at their last meeting.

"She's changed since you've been in Chicago. She's a teacher now. She and Conor are crazy about one another."

Ryan rose, put his coffee cup in the sink, and picked up the ledger. "I have to head back. I've got a long list of people to interview."

"Sure. If you need to talk, you know how to get a hold of me." She wiggled the pink encased smartphone that appeared from her jean pocket.

"You know you're my go-to sis." He gave her a hug and kissed Wally on his curly brown hair.

"Drive safe."

"Always." Ryan unlocked the SUV and slipped into the driver's seat. The engine roared to life as he shook his head. *Lissa and Conor*. Thinking back he should have seen it coming. Their senior year, Conor was home visiting from college for Christmas. Lissa had hung on every word that came out of his older brother's mouth. At the time he'd been just as excited to hear about college life and hadn't thought much about it. And it had been Conor who'd kept him informed of Lissa's whereabouts over the years.

*Enough! I have a murder to solve.*

The four hour drive back to Huckleberry gave him plenty of time to formulate the path of his investigation. Juan, the employee, and Naomi Norton. He'd take the information he gathered from them and decide where to go from there. He'd send the overzealous Blane looking for a blunt but penetrating object in the dumpsters around the gallery.

He kept his mind focused on the investigation until half an hour from Huckleberry when his phone rang. "Greer."

"Hey Ry! Bridget said she told you about Lissa and me." Conor's tone held a bit of hesitation.

"Congratulations. It's about time someone roped you in." As he said the words, they felt genuine and it made him smile. Yep, he could care less that Lissa was marrying his brother.

"You mean that?"

"Yes. I'm glad you both found someone to make you happy." Ryan slowed as he approached the turnoff.

"In that case, would you be my best man? You are the only brother I have, and Mom would twist my ear if I didn't ask you." Conor's joking tone put a lump in Ryan's throat.

They'd been close growing up. Their adult lives had slowly drifted them apart. "Sure. I'd be honored to be your best man."

"Thanks. We appreciate this. And I can hook you up with one of Lissa's bridesmaids."

Ryan cringed. "No thanks. I'll bring my own date."

"You seeing someone Bridget doesn't know about?"

He laughed. His little sister always knew everything about family members. "No. But I met an interesting woman yesterday. I have a feeling we'll be seeing more of each other." His mind flashed his first sight of Shandra Higheagle. He'd felt an instant attraction. Something he hadn't felt in years. *Not since seventh grade.*

"She a suspect?"

"Nope. She found the body, and I'm sure I'll need

to ask her more questions."

"The wedding is August eighteenth."

"That's only two months away. You're moving kind of fast aren't you?"

"We've been dating for two years."

"Two years and no one told me?" Ryan didn't know what hurt worse; the betrayal of his family not telling him, or the fact his brother had been the reason Lissa ignored his calls when he'd returned from Chicago and tried to start up their friendship again.

Conor cleared his throat and croaked. "No one was sure how you'd take it."

"Shit, Conor. I've been in combat and I was nearly killed on American soil by gangs, did you all think I was so fragile I couldn't take you saying you love my ex-girlfriend? What kind of an emotional dork do you think I am?"

"I-we…"

"I'll be there." He ended the conversation and slammed his palm on the steering wheel. Had his mom even kept this a secret? Did the whole family think he was an emotional time bomb?

He whipped the SUV into a parking spot in front of the local police department and sat staring at his reflection in the building's window. He did tend to ignore his family's invitations. And he was lonely. Some nights he ached with need. Not just physically but mentally. He wanted a long marriage, kids, a life that he could look back on and be proud. Like his parents.

A knock on the passenger window made him jump. His gaze focused, and he stared into the pimply face of Blane. The young officer's eyes sparkled with glee, and he had a smirk on his face. Ryan slid the corners of his mouth into a grin. He opened the door and stepped out.

"I need your help on this case. Let's go visit with your chief." He walked ahead of Blane into the station.

Chapter Seven

Shandra couldn't shake the dream that spun in her head into the early morning hours. She'd walked into the lodge on the reservation where the seven drum ceremony was about to take place and found Paula on her hands and knees pleading. Shandra moved deeper into the lodge to see who the gallery owner was talking to and Ella appeared beside Paula. Her grandmother waved a feather over Paula's head and the gallery owner dropped to the ground, red spreading around her.

Shandra had wanted to back out of the lodge, but her feet moved her forward. Ella looked at her. The old woman's eyes shone like two beacons on a dark night. "Greed. It is a Whiteman curse." Then the whole scene faded as drums and chants swirled her around like Dorothy caught in the tornado in the Wizard of Oz.

One cup of coffee did nothing to banish the sleepiness moving her through the morning chores like a zombie. Sheba nudged her hand as Shandra stood, staring into the forest, seeing nothing with her eyes but playing the dream over in her head.

"Why are you coming to me in dreams now, Ella?" She shook her head and shoved away from the corral, heading to her studio.

She spent the morning working up the latest batch of clay she'd brought down the mountain. Usually the process of making the clay pure and usable for throwing was exhilarating. Today, her mind kept wandering to the dream and the person Naomi said entered the gallery right before Paula was killed. There had been lots of tension between Paula and her soon to be ex. "Now he is a widower. How does Sidney feel about his wife's murder?" Her voice rang strong and loud in the big building. Hearing the question set her to wondering who Lil had seen Paula arguing with. Lil knew Sidney, so it couldn't have been him.

Her hands worked less laboriously squeezing water through the clay. The angry motions became more fluid, moving into gentle kneading as her mind wandered to tonight. Sidney was half owner in the Huckleberry Lodge. He'd be at the art event as well as Juan, Paula's assistant and part time artist. "Yes. I think tonight is going to be less of a bore than I'd previously thought."

"You going to the shindig at the Lodge?"

Shandra sprung up from her stool at Lil's voice. The woman moved as quietly as the fluffy orange cat gliding around Lil's lower legs, tail straight in the air like a flagpole.

"Geez, Lil. I wish you'd make a noise so I know you're in the studio." Shandra repositioned her butt on the padded stool and finished the cleaning process on the clay.

"I came through the door like a normal person. What more can I do?"

"Wear bells."

"Now that's foolish. Only a lead cow or goat wears a bell so the rest of the herd can hear and follow her."

Shandra glanced Lil's direction and shook her head. They'd had this unusual relationship for two years, and she still wasn't used to the woman's down home logic and undying devotion to animals and the ranch.

"You didn't answer my question. You going to the Lodge tonight?"

"Yes. Ted and Naomi would expect me to be there since one of my pieces is in the silent auction. And there are a couple of people I need to discuss Paula's death with."

Lil shuddered. "It ain't a good idea to talk of the dead when they didn't die of natural causes."

"If I'm going to find information to get the detective to look somewhere other than at Naomi, I have to talk to people about Paula." She wiped the clay from her fingers, watching the other woman move slow and steady toward the kiln where three vases had cooled enough to be removed. "What did the man you saw quarreling with Paula look like?"

Lil frowned and said, "He had white hair and was dressed fancy. Not like an artist, more like the people who buy your pottery."

Shandra put the clay in a plastic bucket and sealed the top with plastic and a wide rubber band.

"You gonna work in here today?" Lil asked, lifting a vase out of the kiln.

"No. I just wanted to get this bucket of clay worked up." She placed the bucket under a shelf holding coasters with etchings of Huckleberry Mountain. She made the coasters for the souvenir shops in town.

"I need to refine the sketches for my new design." Her hand on the studio door, she glanced over her shoulder at Lil. "I'll glaze those pieces tomorrow, please put them on the glazing table."

"Don't get too nosy at that party tonight. You know bad things happen in threes." Lil carried the vase into the glazing room, her comment skittered a shiver down Shandra's back.

~*~

The remainder of the day, Shandra sat in her screened-in porch sketching and erasing. Her mind wasn't thinking creatively. Her thoughts circled around and around how to keep Naomi away from Detective Greer until the real murderer was found. She knew in her heart her friend didn't kill anyone but there was so much that pointed to her, Shandra's stomach pitched and ached.

The only way to get to the bottom of it would be at the event tonight. And the way to catch a fish was to use an attractive lure. She knew just the dress to wear to catch the roving eye of Sidney Doring and persuade some information out of Juan Lida.

~*~

Ryan found Juan Lida attempting to enter the back door of the Doring Gallery.

"Didn't you see the crime tape at the front door?" Ryan asked, holding his hand on the door latch.

The Hispanic man sent him a scowl and didn't say a word as Ryan motioned for him to enter the building.

The suspect appeared just as Dr. Porter had described him. Anti-social, a bit insolent, and secretive.

"Go to the office. I have some questions for you."

The man's stride faltered at the mention of the office. Was that because he didn't want to relive a murder he committed or because he had something else to hide?

Ryan pulled the tape off the office door, glad to see it hadn't been tampered with and walked through, watching Lida's face.

Juan's gaze went to the desk chair. His Adam's apple bobbed as he swallowed. Tears glistened in his eyes, before he squeezed them shut then opened them and scanned the desk.

"When did you hear about your employer's death?" Ryan pulled out his notepad and started to take notes. He wanted answers and hopefully information that would implicate this person. By interviewing him as a suspect he'd get nowhere, but treating the man like an aide, he might just get what he needed.

"On the news last night." Lida's thick accent made Ryan strain to hear the words.

"Why weren't you here helping her prepare for the upcoming art event?"

Lida tipped his head side to side like someone loosening tight neck muscles. "Mrs. Doring sent me on an errand for the event."

"What kind of an errand?" Ryan kept his face tilted down, but he peered at the man from under his eyelashes. Lida's skin was taking on a ruddier hue along with the tips of his ears.

"Mrs. Doring had an inkling her soon-to-be ex-husband was trying to undermine her gallery and sent me to talk with some artists she'd heard were paid to not consign their work with her." Lida stepped to the desk and opened the bottom drawer where Ryan had taken the ledger and brochures from. His head jerked up and he stared, wide-eyed at Ryan. "This was a robbery?"

"What makes you think that?" He continued to watch the man rifle through the few items left in the drawer.

"There should be a ledger, brochures, and a fi—" He reached down pulling out another drawer.

"I have the ledger and brochures. I've been trying to make sense of the numbers and system used." He walked over beside the man. "But there wasn't a file in that drawer."

"I didn't…"

"Say file? No, but you said enough and the expression on your face said there was more missing. What was in the file? Did it have anything to do with Joyce Carter?"

Lida swung around, his face scrunched in anger and his compact body heading toward the door. Ryan dropped his pad and grabbed the man's wrist, twisting his arm behind his back and quickly securing a cuff.

"What can you tell me about Joyce Carter's overdose? Did she have some help? Was it you perhaps carrying out one of your employer's 'orders'." The last time he'd had the sensation in his gut that the guy he apprehended would roll, he'd ended up in the hospital, having been lured into a trap.

"I did not live here at that time." The man glared over his shoulder.

"But you know who she was and what happened to

her."

"I saw the file Paula kept in the desk and asked her about it. She said it was her retirement fund."

Ryan spun the man to face him. "Was that file the reason for the large sums of money added to her ledger every month?"

"Yes. She said it would keep us happy and healthy for a long time."

Staring into the man's eyes, he saw what he'd missed before. The glistening tears had been not of remorse but of loss. "You and Paula were…more than employee and employer?"

"She taught me the strategy of a gallery owner. I created works of art for her to sell. And together, we were building a bond that could not be broken. One stronger than money or art. One that would transcend time."

Ryan rolled his eyes. This sucker thought Paula loved him. From what he'd learned so far about the woman, she only loved one thing. Money. He uncuffed Lida and motioned for them to leave the office. They walked five feet from the office door and the back door of the building flew open. Blane stood in the doorway, waving something in his hands.

Chapter Eight

Shandra pulled her Jeep up to the entrance of the lodge and slid out, handing her key over to the valet. She wanted to be a bit late and make an entrance so she'd have the attention of everyone, but especially Sidney Doring.

She fluffed the brightly colored tiered skirt and loosened the drawstring on the peasant top enough to draw the neckline all the way to the ends of her shoulders, giving the appearance she didn't wear a bra. She pushed upwards on the bustier under her top, forcing her girls to show themselves a bit at the neckline. If this didn't hook the bait she was after, then she'd misread all her other encounters with Sidney Doring. Everything she'd heard and seen, he was a womanizer who couldn't let an unattached female stay that way for long.

Inside the lodge, she scanned the large foyer filled

with artwork and people. Her nerves zinged and bunched anticipating the task she'd set out to do.

A hand waved in the air. Her gaze followed the arm and spotted Ted and Naomi. With them was a woman who had purchased one of her etched vases the previous year. Shandra set her lips in a gracious smile and wove her way through the crowd to her friends.

"Shandra, you remember Ethel Mayer, don't you?" Naomi's overenthusiastic greeting, shot Shandra's gaze to her friend's face.

"Of course. It's good to see you, Mrs. Mayer. Are you and your husband here on vacation?" Shandra wanted to hurry through the pleasantries and drag her friend into an alcove to question her. She'd never seen Naomi so falsely animated.

"Yes, I told Harold we had to reserve our month here to coincide with this fun art event. After all, I need to add more of your work to my collection." Mrs. Mayer slipped her arm through Shandras. "Tell me about this new look you're working on." She leaned close to Shandra's ear. "I'm determined to win the silent auction piece and buy one of those fabulous gourd-shaped pieces I saw in the magazine article."

Shandra's heart felt both heavy and light. "Since reconnecting with my paternal grandmother, my pieces have become more Native American. Since her passing, I have become even more emotionally tied to my work."

The woman nodded and gave respectful answers, but Shandra's gaze kept returning to Naomi. Why was her friend so jumpy?

"Mrs. Mayer, may I steal Miss Higheagle away from you for a moment?"

Shandra couldn't believe her luck. The lure must have worked. She turned to Sidney Doring and smiled. "Mr. Doring. Mrs. Mayer is purchasing one of my pieces what do you have to offer that could pull me away from her?"

"I am also interested in one of your pieces." His gaze moved leisurely down from her face and remained at the tops of her breasts at the low neckline of her top.

Inside her stomach soured, but on the outside she smiled and slipped her arm through his.

"Mrs. Mayer, I'll find you later to talk more. If I can persuade Sidney to buy one of my vases and place it in the foyer for his guests to see, I would consider this a very successful evening."

Ethel smiled and waved them off.

Sidney drew her away from the crowd and down the hallway toward banquet rooms. She cast a look over her shoulder and locked gazes with Detective Greer.

*Damn!* She wanted to question Sidney but was fearful of leaving Naomi alone with the detective.

"Where are we going Sidney? My artwork is out there." She pointed back toward the foyer.

"Sweetheart, you have been teasing me since you arrived in Huckleberry. I think it's time we see how well we could work together." He pulled her toward him as he backed into a room. *A dark room.*

"I find it a bit slimy that not twenty-four hours after your wife is found dead you're seducing me." Her words had the icy effect she'd hoped for.

Sidney grabbed her arms tighter. "We were in the middle of a divorce. That woman spread her legs for any man she thought would pad her bank account or move her up in business circles. So why shouldn't I have some fun."

"Her death leaves more money in your bank account doesn't it?"

The minute her comment slipped out she regretted it. The hand he swung came fast and with stinging accuracy, snapping her head to the side.

"Ms. Higheagle, would you like to press assault charges?"

The deep, calm voice she heard helped lessen the sting in her cheek. She peered around her hand pressed to her cheek. Detective Greer had Sidney's arms pinned behind his back.

She glanced at Sidney. More than anger sizzled in the air between them. He had the gall to think she wouldn't press charges. She saw it in the smug glimmer in his eyes. Not only would it teach the man a lesson, it would get rid of the detective before he could talk with Naomi.

"Yes, I would like to press charges. Mr. Doring, you may be grieving your wife but that is no reason to hit a woman."

The man stared daggers at her as the detective pulled out handcuffs, securing Sidney's hands behind his back.

"This is preposterous. You can't haul me off in handcuffs. I own this place. I can't be seen—"

"You should have thought of that before hitting this woman." Detective Greer pushed Sidney against the wall and slid a cell phone from his jacket pocket.

Shandra kept her hand over her cheek, wishing this was the corridor to the kitchen and some ice. The detective's voice drew her attention. He looked as good in a western cut suit jacket, Levis, and shiny black cowboy boots as he had the day before in working clothes.

He finished his phone call, and Shandra realized she was staring when he peered into her eyes and grinned like a man with a winning lottery ticket.

"You should get some ice on that." He lowered her hand. His eyes narrowed a moment before he lifted his phone.

"What are you doing?" She raised her hand to hide the cheek.

"I need a photo for evidence." He once again, only gentler, drew her hand away from her face and snapped two photos of her. "Where's the kitchen?"

"On the other side of the foyer." She looked that direction and spotted Naomi and Ted. Their appearance jogged her memory of her goal. "Don't you need to take Sidney to jail?"

"No, I have your favorite police officer coming for him."

Chapter Nine

The look of panic on Shandra's face would have been comical if Ryan had believed it was about facing Officer Blane again. No, her gaze had flicked toward the foyer and then back toward him before she masked the emotion with a smile.

"Did you instruct him on proper apprehending when coming upon a person?" Her smile wasn't genuine.

"We had a discussion about that and other things." Ryan peered out into the crowd. "Do you have a friend I can send over to sit with you while I find ice for your cheek?"

Her glance darted to the man who'd hit her, and then out into the crowd. "Yes. If you'll take Sidney away, I'd like to have Naomi Norton sit with me for a bit."

He nodded toward the crowd. "Which one is she?"

Shandra pointed to a tall, slender blonde who fidgeted with a button on her sweater.

Ryan took hold of Doring and pushed him toward the foyer. Of course, hauling one of the owners through the event was going to cause chaos, but it would also divert suspicion from his investigation.

Doring dug in his feet when they hit the end of the hallway, but eventually, just hung his head and walked as Ryan propelled him toward Mrs. Norton.

When Shandra had called the man Mr. Doring, Ryan couldn't believe his good fortune. The man was on his list to speak to about the murder victim. Now he had Doring in custody and could speak to him after he finished here. He caught a glimpse of the nervous woman Ms. Higheagle requested sit with her. He kept his face a blank canvas but inside he was smiling. One more person from his list he planned to investigate. And she would be present while he took Shandra's statement. He mentally patted himself on the back for coming to this event.

He'd gone back and forth over the pros and cons of investigating in the midst of such an event and decided it was the perfect way to see how his suspects interacted and to see Shandra Higheagle again.

His first impression of Naomi Norton said she was high-strung. He walked up and cleared his throat. She jumped and spun his way, her eyes wide and scared. He'd met a lot of killers, and he didn't think this woman had the strength in her skinny arms to plunge a blunt object through a rib cage. But when adrenaline was gushing and emotions were high, anyone was capable of anything.

"Mrs. Norton?"

"Y-yes?"

"Your friend, Shandra, would like you to sit with her in one of the rooms down the hall." He looked back toward the hall. Shandra stood in the shadows of the hallway.

"What happened?" Her gaze shot to Doring.

"Doring assaulted her."

"Why?" The one word came out in a croak.

Before he could answer, the woman was weaving her way through the crowd to her friend.

A commotion at the entrance drew his attention. Blane rushed into the event as if Ryan'd called in a bomb threat. The young man really needed to learn tact.

Ryan moved across the room toward the officer. When they met, Blane whistled.

"You know who you have here?" he asked.

"Yes. Take him to the station, write him up on assault charges, and hold him until I can ask him some questions. I'll stay here and get the victim's statement."

"You might want to come with me to the car." Blane leaned close and lowered his voice. "Right as you called I found more pictures and things in the dumpster behind the donut shop."

Could this be the missing file? Ryan pushed Doring toward the entrance. He was getting more breaks this evening than he'd expected.

~*~

Shandra hugged Naomi when she arrived. She'd never been hit by a man. It scared her more than she wanted to admit to the detective and herself.

"What happened?" Naomi asked, pulling out of the embrace and touching Shandra's cheek.

"I planned to ask Sidney questions about his wife,

but he got too friendly. I spat out an accusation and he slapped me hard." Tears burned behind her eyes. She blinked to keep them from spilling. Humiliation mixed with the fright and the anger.

"I'm sorry. You shouldn't be playing detective, you could get yourself hurt worse." Naomi led her down the hallway to a couple of chairs. "Do you want me to get some ice?"

"Detective Greer is bringing some." She peered over Naomi's shoulder but couldn't see the detective. She returned her gaze to her friend. "You need to stop fidgeting. You look nervous which makes you look guilty of something."

"I know. I'm trying, but all I can think about is talking to Juan to see if he's said anything about giving me a key to the gallery."

Shandra's heart raced. "No! Don't approach him and don't bring it up. He may have forgotten he even gave you one."

"It wasn't that long ago. He's bound to remember." Naomi lowered her face into her hands. "I can't do this. I should just tell the detective everything."

"I think that would be a good idea."

Shandra's neck popped as she jerked her head to look up at the voice. *Damn!* Poor timing. Detective Greer stood over them holding a clear plastic baggie of ice. He handed it to her and knelt next to Naomi.

"Mrs. Norton, now would be a good time to tell me what you want to get off your conscience." His soothing voice didn't fool Shandra.

"Naomi, you haven't done anything wrong. There isn't any reason—"

Detective Greer shot her a glare. "Mrs. Norton are

you the one who tossed a file about your sister into the dumpster behind the donut shop?"

Shandra couldn't stop her friend's reaction. Naomi shot to her feet as if to run, then dropped into the chair and cried into her hands.

"Are you happy?" Shandra spat at the detective. "It's taken her months to get over her sister's death, and you bring it up with about as much tact as a rhino in rut." Shandra put an arm around her friend. "I don't want you asking her any more questions until you get her husband over here." She leveled an unwavering glare on the detective.

He sighed and rose to his feet. "If you try to sneak her out of here while I get the husband, I'll find you both and haul you in for obstruction of justice."

She continued to glare at him.

"Am I clear?"

"Yes." Shandra wanted to keep glaring at him, but as he walked away she had to admit, he could have pressed Naomi for information. He didn't have to bring in more reinforcements for the woman he wanted to interrogate.

"I have to tell him. It's making me sick holding it in," Naomi said between sobs.

"I know. I hope this detective has enough sense to know you didn't do it." Shandra glanced up and watched Detective Greer and Ted walk down the hall toward them. The detective had a determined jut to his chin. Ted's face was slack with worry.

She stood, allowing Ted to take the chair next to his wife. Shandra tugged on Detective Greer's sleeve, drawing him a short distance from the two.

He peered down at her, waiting.

Clearing the lump that all of a sudden appeared in her throat, she opened her mouth to speak.

His eyes narrowed, and she snapped her jaw shut. What if he didn't believe her?

"Do you have something to tell me about yesterday afternoon, Ms. Higheagle?"

She'd take the offensive. "I didn't lie to you yesterday. I just withheld a detail until I'd asked Naomi a question."

"And that detail was...?"

She glanced at her friend. She'd stopped crying. Her red swollen eyes peered at her and she nodded.

Releasing her angst on a whoosh of air, she looked into the detective's dark brown eyes. "When I parked in front of the Doring Gallery yesterday I saw Naomi crossing the side street."

Her relief at telling the truth was short lived when he pulled a small notepad out of his jacket pocket.

"She's not a suspect. She wouldn't kill anyone."

Those dark brown eyes narrowed, and an eyebrow rose as he scribbled on the pad. "I'll be the judge of who is a suspect." He glanced up. "I'm impartial."

"What does that mean?" Shandra crossed her arms. It wasn't until the detective's gaze drifted downward that she realized her actions had exposed more of her girls than she usually did in public. She grabbed the string, drawing it up, and tying a large bow. The neckline resided where a modest woman would wear it.

His gaze returned to her face. "It means, I'm not friends with Mrs. Norton, giving me an impartial perspective."

"Detective, my wife is ready to tell you everything." Ted held Naomi's hand and waved them over with his free hand.

Shandra started toward the couple. A hand on her arm stopped her. She peered up into the detective's eyes and saw a hint of empathy.

"Don't interrupt. Let her tell her story. Then I'll ask you both questions." His deep voice was only loud enough for the two of them to hear. If it had been under different circumstances she would have found it seductive.

When she didn't answer and continued to stare into his eyes, he smiled. *Ooo*. She had to stop getting sucked into his gaze. He wasn't here to help Naomi.

"Are you going to interrupt?" His tone proved he saw rebellion in her eyes.

"No."

"Go—"

"As long as you don't interrogate her like a criminal." Shandra shook off his hand, still resting on her arm and stood beside her friend.

Chapter Ten

Ryan couldn't believe the audacity of the Higheagle woman. She was telling him how to do an interrogation. He didn't plan to make the Norton woman cry, but if she started tearing up while telling her side of things there was nothing he could do about it. He ran a hand over the muscles bunching in the back of his neck and directed his attention to the woman with red-rimmed eyes, clutching her husband's hand like a lifeline.

"Mrs. Norton, we found photos in a dumpster behind the donut shop. The woman in the photos was identified as your sister. Did you have anything to do with tossing those photos in the dumpster?" Movement to the woman's right, told him Ms. Higheagle wasn't happy with his direct questioning. But this was his investigation not hers. He'd never let another person influence his train of thought, but his mind wandered to the glimpse he'd received of the woman's attributes when she'd tried to get huffy with him. He started to smile before dragging his mind back to the suspect he was questioning.

"Mrs. Norton. I'm being kind by questioning you with your husband and friend present. I could take you to the police station and ask you these questions in a room with just the two of us."

Her head shook and her eyes widened. "No, please. I don't want to do this alone."

"Then answer my question."

Her husband nudged her. "Go on Naomi, tell him about the file."

Her blue eyes filled with tears as she began to speak in a shaky voice. "I've had a suspicion there was more to Joyce's death than an overdose. She was off drugs and proud of it. I thought it was suspicious that Paula held such a dislike for my sister. They'd never met until Joyce applied for the assistant's job." She drew in a breath. "Paula made a comment at one of the art events that I'd be surprised what all she knew about my sister." Her voice grew stronger. "That made me curious about what she could have." She drew in another breath, looked at her husband, and started in. "I knew Paula took her lunch from one to two every day and there was usually no one in the gallery. I paid her assistant Juan to make me a copy of her back door key."

Ryan peered at the woman. "How did you know he wouldn't tell Paula?"

She blushed and her eyelids lowered. "I threatened to turn him into INS. We were investigated a couple years ago for hiring an immigrant. I looked Juan up when he got the job over Joyce and learned he is an illegal." She turned to her husband who stared at her in disbelief. "I know you told me to let things go, but I can't believe Joyce killed herself with drugs. I just can't."

Ryan jotted down the information about Juan. "You used the key the day Mrs. Doring was killed?"

"Yes. I waited for her to leave, then I went in the back door and looked through the drawers in her desk. That's when I found the file." She squeezed her eyes shut and shuddered. "The photos were awful! I can't believe Joyce would have exposed herself like that without being out of her mind on drugs. It was her worthless boyfriend who talked her into taking them."

The last declaration was the first glimpse he'd had of any fire or anger in the woman. He could envision it building and escalating as she looked at the photos he'd skimmed through at Blane's cruiser a few minutes earlier. They were not photos you would want any of your family to see.

"It made you angry to see those photos and know that Paula held on to them." The color deepened in her cheeks.

"Yes." Ryan said, "Why was she holding them? There wasn't any reason I could think of."

Mrs. Norton glared at him. "I took them, because knowing Paula, she'd probably pull them out and have a good laugh knowing my sister had stooped that low."

Other thoughts were twisting around in Ryan's head. What if the photos were behind the large sums of money added to Paula's books every month? He sized up the Nortons. Did they make enough to pay that amount every month? It would be reason to steal the photos. He made a note to check their financials.

"Did Paula return before you left?"

A cough to his right, drew his gaze to Ms. Higheagle who shook her head and glared. He returned the glare and directed his attention back at Mrs. Norton.

"Did you confront her?"

Naomi's face turned white. "No! I heard the buzz at the front door and grabbed the folder. I headed to the back of the gallery and out the back door. I ran down the alley and tossed the file into the dumpster behind the donut shop. When I looked up, the back door of the gallery was closing. I know it closed behind me, so someone else must have entered. I bought donuts and returned to our gallery through the alley. That was when Shandra saw me."

He turned his attention to Ms. Higheagle. "Did you see anyone besides Mrs. Norton?"

"No, but my caretaker, Lil, said she saw Paula and a man with white hair arguing behind the Quik Mart the day before Paula was killed." Ms. Higheagle's lips were drawn up into a satisfied smile. Her eyes seemed to taunt him with "I can discover clues, too."

"Did this Lil get a good enough look to pick him out if we come up with a line up?"

"I'll ask her. If she can describe him, I'll make a drawing."

He stared at her. "I thought you made things from clay."

A smirk tipped her lips. "I do the etchings on my vases and draw up ideas. In art school I dabbled in portraits."

This woman not only had a keen intelligence, she was multi-talented. The more he knew about her the more intrigued he became.

He pulled his mind away from where his thoughts

were headed and peered at Mrs. Norton. "What can you tell me about the boyfriend that got your sister hooked on drugs?"

"Joyce met Dale Young five years ago. He claimed to be a painter, but later we discovered the only money that passed through his hands came from drugs." Mrs. Norton glanced at her husband. He nodded and she drew in a breath as Ryan jotted down the boyfriend's name.

"When Joyce stopped returning my calls after living with Dale for a year, I went to Seattle to see if she was okay. Dale refused to let me see Joyce and threatened me if I ever came around there again." The woman's hands shook. "That's when I urged Ted to let me have a private investigator see what was going on. He reported that Joyce was stoned most of the time and seemed to be happy with that life." She shook her head. "When Dale was arrested and she had the chance, Joyce called me and begged me to help her get off the drugs. I went with her to check into rehab. Then she came and lived with us while she was getting her life back together."

Ryan slid a glance toward Ms. Higheagle. The compassion on her face toward her friend was admirable. But that didn't get him any answers.

"Who was the private investigator you used?"

"Terrance Baylor. He's in Seattle. Why do you need to contact him?" Mr. Norton asked.

"I just want to rule out Joyce's death having anything to do with this investigation." Ryan scanned his notes then studied the trio. "Has there always been bad feelings between you and Paula Doring?"

Ms. Higheagle huffed her indignation and pursed

her lips.

Norton glared at him "Why are you asking?"

"I'm trying to figure out why Joyce applied for a job with Paula if there has always been this animosity between the two galleries."

The husband and wife stared at one another. It was clear neither one of them had thought much about why Joyce applied.

"Surely, there were other jobs here that she could have applied for."

Mrs. Norton's brow furrowed. "I remember she came home from applying for jobs and said someone had mentioned there was an opening at Doring Gallery, would I mind if she applied. I knew she was hoping for something more than a waitress job, so I told her to go ahead." The woman's face scrunched up and tears sprouted anew. "Oh God! Did I get her killed?"

Ms. Higheagle dropped to her knees beside her friend and hugged her. "No, you did not kill your sister." Her golden eyes glared at him. "I think it's time you moved on and harassed someone else for a while."

Didn't Ms. Higheagle understand her friend confessed to being in the gallery at the time of the murder? She was his strongest lead. Yet, in his gut he didn't think the woman sobbing in Ms. Higheagle's arms had the wherewithal or the strength to stab with a blunt object.

"That's all for now, but I'll be around to your gallery tomorrow with more questions."

"We'll be there. This is one of our biggest selling weekends." Norton drew his wife to her feet. "Shandra, would you get Naomi cleaned up. They'll be giving away the silent auction items soon."

## Chapter Eleven

Shandra gave Detective Greer one more glare and then helped her friend down the hall to the closest restroom. As much as she wanted to be angry with the detective for questioning Naomi, his questions had her mind going in a million different directions about whether the overdose a year ago and Paula's murder were connected.

She helped Naomi freshen up with a cold water compress of wet paper towels on her red swollen eyes and reapplied the little makeup Naomi wore. Back out in the lobby with the attendees, she noticed Detective Greer questioning Juan Lida. The other person she hoped to question herself. She touched her bruised cheek. Hopefully this conversation wouldn't go as poorly as the one she had with Sidney Doring.

The crowd began to gather around the microphone where the master of ceremonies encouraged people to place their final silent auction bids. "Only five minutes left before we pull the sign-up sheets."

The detective moved away from Juan. Using this chaotic time to her advantage, Shandra sidled up beside Paula's assistant.

"Hi Juan. Did you put anything in the auction?" she asked, watching as his angry gaze on the detective drift to her. A tired smile didn't quite light his eyes.

"I wanted to." His eyes glistened with moisture. He cleared his throat. "I could not take it from the gallery."

"I'm sorry. This must be hard for you after..." She gave Juan her full attention. "I know how closely gallery owners work with their assistants."

"We were more. We were to be married." He choked out the last few words and turned, hurrying through the crowd.

*Married*? Had Juan realized Paula was seeing someone else and killed her in a jealous rage? She'd not witnessed him angry but had heard stories from other artists about his temper. Juan didn't fit the description of the man Lil saw with Paula right before she was killed. Did that person find out she was marrying Juan and kill her out of jealousy? The vision of Paula having more than one man fighting for her affections was laughable. What did men see in her? She was a bully, average looks and body, and her husband had all the money. Of course if the divorce had gone Paula's way...

The master of ceremonies began reading the top bidders on the ten items for silent bids. The vase she'd donated was the fifth item.

"The top bid of two thousand and ten dollars goes to Ryan Greer."

Shandra shook her head. She couldn't have heard

that right. Whether she heard right or not, the detective walked toward her vase.

A volunteer hurried toward her. "We need a photo of you and the winner," the white-haired, older woman said, grasping Shandra's hand in her small boney one and tugging her toward the grinning detective.

Shandra stood on the opposite side of her vase smiling at the camera as her mind raced. *How could a detective afford to buy expensive art? And why would he want her vase?* When the camera person moved on to the next item, winner, and artist, she turned to Detective Greer.

"It's a good cause your money is going to, but why my vase?"

His hand slid over the curve of the vase. His eyes held warmth and a bit of awe in their brown depths. "It's beautiful and I need a wedding gift for my older brother and my ex-girlfriend."

That statement shocked her. Not that he had a girlfriend. That he had an ex and she was marrying his brother. Also the warmth in his statement about the two marrying. She blinked and his grin grew.

"I guess there aren't many men who could be happy the girl they planned to marry the moment he met her in seventh grade was marrying their brother instead."

Shandra had trouble finding her voice. "N-no, I guess not…Seventh grade? You fell in love with this woman in seventh grade and let your brother swipe her?" Her first impression of this man had been his doggedness. Surely someone with his tenacity wouldn't let a woman he loved be taken away.

"It's a long story I'd be willing to share if you'd

care to sit and have a drink with me."

The invitation in his voice and eyes were so unlike the sharpness she'd witnessed as he questioned people. She couldn't help but smile back. "Are you talking about tonight or—"

"Excuse me." The same bird-like older woman who drug her over for a photo shoved between them with a clipboard. "We need either a check, credit card, or information on where to send a bill before you leave."

He shrugged apologetically and pulled out his wallet and spoke to the woman. "How are you taking credit cards?"

"We write it down—"

"Then give me the clip board. I'll send you a check. I don't allow my credit information to be out in the open and neither should you." He took the paperwork and began writing.

Shandra grinned. That was the cop mode she'd witnessed. She was intrigued by the charming man who'd asked her out for a drink and let his first love get away. She'd had a first love but that was a teenage crush. Somehow she didn't think his had been a crush. It sounded like it had lasted. So why had the woman ditched him for his brother? Could his brother be even more handsome and dedicated than Detective Greer?

He handed the paperwork and pen back to the woman and turned to her, his face sliding from business-like to charming again. "Do you have any reason you need to stay any longer?"

"Not really."

"The bar here is open." He motioned for her to go ahead of him through the crowd of art lovers.

Shandra smiled and headed toward the bar. She knew eventually most of this crowd would end up in the bar. By then she hoped to be headed home. The last month had worn her out. Between deadlines for this event, her aunt calling to make sure she came to her grandmother's funeral, and then the dreams filled with her grandmother... It's a wonder she didn't have black bags under her eyes.

She glanced over her shoulder and found the detective right behind her. He reached out a hand, placing it on her lower back. The contact surprised her. He smiled as he navigated her forward and out of the crowd. They walked in silence down the short hall to the bar entrance, his hand still pressed against her as he moved to her side.

"Isn't it bad form for you to be in a bar while on duty?" she asked as he pulled out a chair at a table in the far corner where they could see everyone who entered. There was only a scattering of customers.

"I'm no longer on duty." He smiled as the waitress approached.

"What can I get you two?" The woman asked.

"I'll have the house white wine," Shandra said.

"I'll have iced tea," Detective Greer added and the waitress headed to the bar.

"I thought you weren't on duty?"

"I'm not, but if you're drinking, one of us has to be sober to drive the other home." He leaned back in his chair.

"Do you plan to get me drunk?" She'd only been drunk once in her life. The memory kept her from overindulging.

"No."

"Then you don't have to worry about driving me home. I only have one drink. I don't like to be out of control and more than one drink can make a person say and do stupid things."

He studied her a moment. "I gathered that you don't like to be out of control the first time we met." He leaned forward. "Care to share why?"

"No. You invited me to explain your brother marrying your ex-girlfriend."

"Touché!"

The waitress returned with their drinks. He pulled out his wallet, paid, and slipped it back in his pocket.

Shandra sipped her wine and waited. It was his story, and she had enough Nez Perce blood in her to know a storyteller will tell their story in their own time and in their own way. Her easy patience had annoyed her mother and stepfather. Shandra learned she'd inherited patience the summer she lived with her grandmother.

Detective Greer took a drink of his tea, cleared his throat, and looked at her. "In the seventh grade I fell for Lissa Chambers the minute she walked into English class. I caught her eye, and we were a couple until our high school graduation. At the time I didn't realize I'd lost her to my brother. Looking back now, I see it all clearly."

"So you haven't been a couple, just high school sweethearts?" That didn't make it so bad. That had to have been ten or twelve years ago.

The grimace on his face said there was more.

"Come on, Detective, you can't make a face like that and not tell me more." She laughed.

"Only if you call me Ryan."

She studied his face. Was that a plea in his eyes to forget how they met? "Okay, Ryan. Now tell me the "rest of the story."

"The Christmas break of our senior year my brother was home from college. Lissa and I hung on his every word. At the time I thought her infatuation was because he was telling us what our lives would be like soon. Now, I see that was when she started losing interest in me. When it came time to go to college, she headed to New York to become a model. In anger, I enlisted in the Army. I came back after my enlistment, flew to New York to see her, and she was cold. Acted like I wasn't good enough for her. I used my military background and got on the Chicago police force." He took several swallows of tea and peered over her head. His brow furrowed. She could tell he wasn't seeing anything in the room, but something in his mind.

What could he be seeing? Heart break? Violence? She sipped her wine and waited.

## Chapter Twelve

A roar went up in the lobby. The sound was like a slap to Ryan's brain. He pulled out of the memories of that night in the alley and peered into the waiting face of Shandra Higheagle.

"You're very patient," he commented to stall.

"It's an inherited trait." She sipped her wine and peered at him over the glass.

Was that a challenge to ask her about herself? "From your last name I take it you have Native American in your ancestry."

Her eyes narrowed. "Do you have a problem with that?"

*Ah, a touchy subject.* "Nope. One of my best friends in school was Coeur d'Alene."

Her posture relaxed, and she took another sip.

"What happened in Chicago?" Her voice was low and husky, the tone inquisitive.

Even though she asked an innocent question, the answer was so loaded, he wasn't sure he could answer. Ryan rubbed his hand over the muscles tightening at the base of his neck. The shrink said it would take time for him to be able to talk about what happened. But the more he did, the easier it would be for him to let go of the anger and remorse.

"If it's too much, I don't need to know. After all, I'm a suspect and—"

"No. You're not a suspect."

Her eyes widened, and she set her glass down. "Really? You believe me?"

A grin spread across his face at her incredulous disbelief. "Yes. I ruled you out when I saw the wound. There was no way you could have cleaned every bit of blood off your hands before Officer Blane arrived."

"But Naomi is still a suspect."

The finality in her statement caused him to study her. What made her care so much for the other woman?

"You're an eyewitness to seeing her cross the street right after the murder was committed. Why do you believe she's innocent?"

"Because I know Naomi." Her golden eyes sparked with defiance.

"People don't always show you all their sides." He'd witnessed this on many occasions in his profession. It was his trust in a young man that had put him in the hospital and rehab.

"I was by Naomi's side as she helped her sister recover and after she was found dead. If she had wanted to lash out at someone, that would have been the time. She was beside herself with grief, but she never once threatened or accused anyone. Even knowing the hell the boyfriend had put Joyce through, Naomi didn't vent about hoping he rotted in jail or anything. Not like I did. I couldn't believe the scumbag received such a light sentence."

Ryan snagged onto that bit of information. "What do you mean?"

"He was caught red-handed with enough drugs and weapons violations that he should have been in jail for a long time. But he received a sentence of eighteen months." Shandra took a swallow of her wine and stared daggers at the glass.

Ryan pulled out his notepad and wrote, *Informant?* next to Dale Young's name. He doubted it had anything to do with this case, but he liked to cover all unanswered questions. Glancing at Shandra, he could tell she'd appreciate whatever information he came up with.

"For what it's worth, I'm not convinced Naomi killed Paula. The wound that was inflicted would have required more strength than I think your friend would have even if in a rage when adrenaline can make a body stronger than usual."

He smiled as her expressive face took on a calmer appearance. Her lips twitched into a smile.

"So, you didn't finish telling me how your brother nabbed your girlfriend." She raised an eyebrow quizzically.

He couldn't stop the laugh that bubbled in his chest and up his throat. "Our first meeting I had the feeling you had the determination of a bull dog."

"Thank you. I take homage to our four-legged friends."

"You like dogs?"

"Ahh, you're changing the subject. I won't tell you anything about me until you finish your story."

Ryan's cell phone vibrated. He pulled it out and noted the Huckleberry Police Chief's number. He pushed the button and leaned back in his chair.

"Greer."

"Doring is ranting and raving and shouting legal jargon. You need to get over here and finalize the arrest papers." Chief Sandberg's usually jovial tone wasn't apparent.

"On my way." Ryan pushed the off button and stared at Shandra.

"I have to go write up the paperwork on Doring. Anything you want to charge him with besides assault?

"I wish I could say he murdered his wife, but we don't have proof." Shandra's gaze held his.

This was the first time in a long time that Ryan was reluctant to hurry off to do his job. He would much prefer to stay here gazing into Shandra's eyes and toss barbs back and forth than write up the paperwork on the assault. But he also had a suspect where he could interrogate him.

He stood. "I really have to go. It would be a good idea if you could get the sketch done of the man your housekeeper saw arguing with the victim."

Shandra nodded. "I'll go home and as soon as Lil gets up tomorrow I'll have her describe the man to me." She stepped in front of him. "How do I contact you when I have the sketch done?"

Looking down into her upturned face, he wanted to kiss that smart mouth, but instead he pulled a card out of his jacket pocket and waved it under her nose. He would have preferred sliding the card under the bow on the front of her blouse, but that would have been unprofessional.

He jerked his thoughts away from that image and smiled. "Call when you have the sketch. I'll come get it."

Shandra snatched the card. "Good. I've wasted enough time off my mountain." She spun and headed for the door.

"Your mountain?" He stood, staring after her as she disappeared through the door. He turned to the cocktail waitress picking up their glasses. "What does she mean by 'her mountain'?"

"She owns a thousand acres of the backside of Huckleberry Mountain."

Ryan tucked the information away and walked down the hallway and into the lobby. He spotted the Nortons and altered his direction.

Ted had an arm around his wife's shoulder, their heads bent together talking quietly.

Standing in front of the couple, he felt like an interloper but had a question the two could answer. "What happens to the art in the Doring Gallery?" Ryan wondered when the artists would come to collect their work. He'd like to size each one up. When he'd talked with Juan earlier the man had refused to answer any questions. Ryan thought a good scare might do the man some good. Haul him into the station and threaten to call INS.

"Sidney will either keep it open or have the artists come pick up their pieces." Ted turned to the door.

"Mr. Doring was a part owner in the gallery?" He hadn't noted anything about a partnership in the papers and files he'd read.

Ted looked puzzled. "He was married to Paula so I assumed he was."

One more thing to look into. "Good night." Ryan pulled out his notepad and scribbled as he headed for the door. He was getting more questions than answers.

Chapter Thirteen

As soon as the sun filtered through the pines, Shandra headed to the barn. Lil's morning routine was the same, rain, snow, or sunshine. At this time of day, she made coffee in an old aluminum pot on a one-burner hot plate and ate a bowl of oatmeal in the tack room where she slept. Shandra had offered the woman a room in the house or one above the studio, but Lil had been sleeping in the tack room for most of her adult life and that was where she wanted to stay.

Shandra opened the small door on the barn and slipped in, making Sheba wait for her outside. The interior was dark, but the light shining from the open door of the tack room guided her way. She stood a moment outside the room watching Lil pour a cup of coffee and pet the fluffy cat, Lewis. What made a person live such a solitary life with only a cat and spend seventy percent of her time caring for animals?

She knocked on the door frame. "Can I come in?"

Lil spun, spilling her coffee over her hand. "Shit

and corn cobs. Why did you scare me like that?" The woman scolded as she wiped at the spill with a towel.

"I'm sorry. I didn't mean to scare you." Shandra felt like she had the time she came across her mother and stepfather in a passionate embrace. Embarrassed and regretting coming into Lil's space. The woman would have been at the studio in an hour, and Shandra could have talked to her then. But she was anxious to get started on the drawing. It could prove to be the murderer. While Detective Greer, Ryan said he didn't believe Naomi could have committed the murder, she didn't doubt he still had her on the list of suspects.

"What brings you to the barn so early? You going on a morning ride?" Lil picked up the pot and motioned to an extra cup that hung from one of the two pegs on the wall above her makeshift counter.

After startling the woman, having a cup of coffee with her was the least she could do. "That sounds good. I didn't get to coffee yet." Shandra sat in one of the chairs alongside a small wooden table that looked like it could have been a wedding gift to Lil's grandparents.

Lil handed her the full cup and took the only other chair in the small room. A single bed stood along the opposite wall. "So what brought you out here so early?"

"I told Detective Greer that you had witnessed Paula arguing with a man. He asked me to do a sketch from how you describe the man." Shandra didn't want to pin too much hope on this being the man who killed Paula, but it was the only thing they had.

Lil bobbed her head. "I can tell you what he looked like. They were there for long enough I got a good look."

Shandra sipped the coffee, remembering how

strong the older woman liked to make it. The one sip was strong, bitter, and curled her nose hairs. "I'll go get my drawing supplies and meet you in the studio." She stood with the cup in her hand. "I'll bring this to the studio with me."

"I'll be right there after I check on the horses." Lil swallowed the rest of her coffee in one long gulp.

Shandra cringed inwardly and left the barn. Sheba bound across the expanse from the tree line to her. At the house, she poured out the strong coffee and refilled her cup with her own milder brew. A flutter of anticipation tickled her stomach. She could very well be sketching a murderer. This could be an integral piece of information. The notion gave her the same satisfaction and a touch more pride than when she saw a finished vase shiny with glaze.

Grabbing up a bag she'd filled earlier with a sketch pad, pencils, and eraser, she headed out to the studio. Shandra arrived before Lil and set about taking vases out of the kiln before refilling it with the latest souvenir items she planned to take to the local stores. Sheba sprawled in her usual place under the glazing table. As the dog grew, Shandra had taught Sheba to go straight under the table when she entered the studio.

Lil arrived, making the process of loading the small pieces go faster. Once the coasters were in the kiln and it was set, they moved to the chairs in the stream of light coming through one of the front windows. Shandra settled into her cushioned arm chair she sat in to draw or ponder what she should make next. Lil sat on an industrial folding chair.

"What was the shape of his head?" Shandra asked to get the process started.

"Masculine."

Shandra raised an eyebrow. "As opposed to?"

"He had the squarish, manly type of head. Square chin, square jaw, flat cheeks, and block shaped head."

"Good." Shandra made decisive but light lines. "Like this?" She showed the drawing to Lil.

"Yeah, only the head's too square and the face too wide. More of a triangle, I guess."

The process took two hours before Lil was satisfied with the outcome. Shandra peered into the face she'd created. *Have I seen you before?* He looked vaguely familiar. "But where?"

"What?" Lil asked.

"Nothing, I was talking to myself." She pulled Ryan's card out of her back jean pocket and her cell phone out of her denim shirt pocket. "I better call the detective and let him know we have a sketch ready."

Lil grunted and headed out the door. It was Sunday. Lil would make her pilgrimage up the mountain on her old mare, Sunshine. Shandra hadn't asked where she went or why, but every Sunday, weather permitting, the two went up the mountain and didn't return until an hour before dark. Just one more quirk of her stray she'd yet to figure out.

"Detective Greer."

A smile tipped up the corners of Shandra's mouth at the sound of Ryan's voice. The minute she realized the correlation, she instantly furrowed her brows.

"This is Shandra Higheagle. I have the sketch we talked about last night." She used a business-like tone.

"I'd know your voice anywhere." The suggestiveness in his voice made her smile.

She bit down on her lower lip to keep from

slipping into the flirtatious banter he was opening up. "Are you still interested in the sketch?"

"Yes. I'll be there in thirty minutes."

She laughed. "Do you even know where I live?"

"I googled the address last night." His tone indicated he took her question as an affront.

"Where are you?" It would take him a good forty-five minutes from Huckleberry to get here He had to have spent the night in town to be able to get here even that fast.

"At the Huckleberry police station."

"You must be dedicated." She didn't know where he lived, but she was certain it wasn't in Huckleberry or she would have run into him before now.

"Huckleberry is where the murder took place and where all the suspects are. I'm not leaving until this is solved."

"Is that a siren I hear?"

"I told you I'd be there in thirty." The line went dead.

Shandra shook her head and couldn't stop the smile that twitched at her lips.

~*~

Ryan bumped up the narrow dirt road in his SUV and wondered if he'd made a wrong turn. In his haste to see the woman and get his hands on the only lead he had for this case, he'd scribbled the directions down in what his sisters called his chicken gumbo. The bouncy road made it even harder to read his scratches on the notepad. While he'd made good time on the paved county road, he had to slow down considerably to keep from dislodging the items stashed in his vehicle.

The Tahoe eased out of the trees. In the middle of a

picturesque meadow sat a log house, and two barn-red buildings. He spotted Shandra's copper colored Wrangler and knew he was in the right place. He rolled to a stop in front of the cedar split-rail fence. A dog the size of a Shetland pony with a head the size of a mountain lion came loping around the side of the house. The markings resembled a tri-color border collie, but the body shape and shaggy hair didn't resemble any dog he'd ever seen.

"Hey there!" he said in his most obliging tone as he stepped out of the vehicle. Would Shandra leave a vicious dog loose knowing he was coming? He smiled. Depended on her mood.

The dog crouched and approached in such a comical stealthy move for such a large animal that Ryan couldn't stop the laughter that burst forth.

"Are you laughing at my guard dog?"

He looked up. Shandra stood on the porch, her arms crossed, but her face reflected the mirth he felt.

"You have to admit, he/she—"

"She. Her name is Sheba."

"Hi Sheba." He scratched the fluffy ears and was rewarded with a slobbery lick. "She might look scary at first but that crawl will have any bad guy rolling on the ground yucking it up."

"All I need is the first impression to stop them. By the time they realize she's a marshmallow, I'll have my forty-five aimed at them." Shandra pivoted. "Come on in. I have fresh coffee made." She threw over her shoulder. "It was fresh. You said you'd be here in thirty minutes."

The laughter in her voice made him grin rather than toss a reply. He crossed the small green patch of grass onto the stepping stones he recognized as being something Shandra had made. There wasn't any mistaking the color of the stones or the etching he'd learned was her handy work on the coasters at the police station.

He'd expected the house to be sparse and hold only necessities. The first step in told him Shandra enjoyed being surrounded by art and inspirations. The woven rug on the tile entry had vivid colors and intricate geometric designs. A huge painting of horses hung on the wall at the stair landing. The furniture was dark, carved, and heavy. She led him through the living room accented with vibrant colors in throws and pillows on leather overstuffed couch and chairs. The large fireplace had a painting of an elderly Native American above the massive wood mantel.

"I thought we'd sit in here. It's my favorite room." Shandra stopped at a breakfast nook with three sides wall-to-ceiling windows. The view was spectacular.

"This has to be inspiring." He stood with his back to the rest of the house and peered out the windows to the meadow, stretching to the trees, and towered over by a mountain. A herd of deer walked into the meadow, the grass up to their knees and colorful early summer wildflowers adding color to the swaying meadow grass.

"It is. I do most of my drawing here in this light and with this to remind me how beautiful this earth is." She placed two cups of coffee on the table and sat.

Ryan took the seat across the table from her. He had his first good look at the bruise on her cheek. He reached across the table and gently ran his thumb over the purple splotches from the hand print. "You need to come to the police station and sign the formal complaint." His gut tightened as his mind rewound the scene he'd witnessed last night. What other damage would the man have done if he hadn't intervened?

She sat back away from his reach. "I'll go down later this afternoon. I have to finish a firing I'm doing before I can go anywhere. Lil could pull the coasters out, but I'm using a new process. She won't know the right moment to pull them. And she's up on the mountain."

"What's she doing up there?" He pulled his thoughts from the night before and back to the here and now.

"I don't know. She rides her horse up the mountain every Sunday. She says she gets closer to God to do her Sunday worship." She smiled and shrugged. "With Lil, for all I know, she gets naked and dances. She is different, but I wouldn't be able to live up here without her."

Shandra shoved a sketch book across the table. "This is the man she saw arguing with Paula."

Ryan picked up the book, opened the cover and stared. "Wow."

"Do you know him?" Her voice rose with excitement.

"No. You are really good." He glanced up and caught her blushing. Didn't she realize the talent she had?

"I just drew what Lil said he looked like. Will you take that to the resort and ask around?"

"That's where I'm headed straight from here. I'm surprised you aren't down in the middle of all the buying frenzy that was going on this morning. I couldn't walk down the streets all the galleries are on without running into someone carrying something." He took a sip of the coffee and sighed. It wasn't bitter like the stuff they were giving him at the Huckleberry P.D.

"I did my duties on Friday and Saturday. Now, it's back to business as usual."

"Does that mean holing up on your mountain?" He scanned the room and the serenity outside the windows. Not a bad place to hide away.

"Pretty much. I don't have another show for two months. Then I'll take a week to pack up the merchandise going to the show and be gone for a week." She stared out the windows. "If I could find someone to do the shows, I'd never leave my mountain."

"You could survive without the glitz and glamour like last night?" He had a feeling she would be happy to slip into the mountain. She dressed to catch attention but that wasn't the real Shandra. The woman with her hair pulled up and secured with one of those plastic claw-like things, a large denim shirt over the top of a light blue t-shirt and worn-out jeans looked more comfortable than the siren that attended the event last night. He had to admit both versions were attractive.

"I grew up on a cattle ranch in Montana. I like the solitary life, but I can glam it up now and then to help sell the craft that allows me to live the way I like." She took a sip of her coffee and peered at him over the cup rim.

"A couple hundred years ago we'd have been enemies." He chuckled when she spit coffee.

Chapter Fourteen

"Excuse me?" Shandra couldn't believe he was that racist after proclaiming his best friend in school was Native American.

"My family comes from a long line of sheep ranchers."

Ryan's eyebrow raised as if he knew exactly where her thoughts had shot to. She'd never been this sensitive about her roots until Ella's death and her nightly visits in Shandra's dreams.

"Yes, I've heard many tales of the wars between cattle and sheep ranchers." She had to readjust her thoughts. Did he say that to specifically goad her?

"My parents still dabble in the sheep industry, but all my siblings left the ranch and have made lives that have nothing to do with the field maggots."

Again his comment confused her. "Field maggots?"

He laughed. "That's the term those who don't look

on sheep favorably call them."

"Oh." She stared into his dark brown eyes. He was having fun with her lack of knowledge or with the fact he'd completely rattled her with his earlier comment. Two could play that game.

"Did you know Juan Lida was going to marry Paula Doring?"

"He made that statement to me last night. But I'm thinking the woman wasn't ready to get caught up in another marriage so soon. I had to go put in my final bid on your vase before I could ask him about the large sums of money entered into the ledger the beginning of every month."

Shandra sat up and leaned toward him. "Paula was getting large sums of money?" She settled back in her chair and thought. "It had to be from her husband. I know he was a silent partner in the gallery."

This time Ryan leaned forward. "With the divorce, do you think he would continue to put money into the gallery?"

Shandra tried to pull up conversations she'd had with Paula. Her grandmother's whispered words slipped through her mind. *Greed. It is a Whiteman curse.*

"I can't see Sidney giving her a cent once they separated. He would have wanted to use that money to lure the next conquest."

"So they both had roving eyes?"

"That's putting it mildly. I never understood why they stayed married as long as they did. From the first gallery event at Doring Gallery anyone with half a brain could see they were flirting with other people and completely ignoring one another." She'd never understood why people married if they had a roving nature. She scowled. Like her stepfather. Her mother wouldn't listen or refused to hear about it. That relationship had soured her on matrimony. Though watching Ted and Naomi was weakening her defenses a bit.

Ryan pulled out his notepad and wrote, or more precisely from what she could see, scribbled.

"What are you writing down?"

He glanced up, his brow furrowed as though in thought. "It's police business."

"You're asking me questions to help the investigation. Maybe I can answer whatever it is you wrote down."

A smile twitched at his lips. "I am asking you questions as a witness. There's a difference between that and giving away case confidentiality."

While he said she wasn't a suspect, he was still withholding information. How was she going to keep Naomi clear of his investigation if he didn't tell her what he was thinking?

"I see. Then I guess you really don't need my help. So I'll just take my sketch back." She reached across the table to grab the sketch.

Ryan caught her hand before it landed on the paper. "No, this is now police evidence. If you want a copy, make another sketch."

His hand held hers gently but firmly. It was warm, strong, and slightly calloused. She glanced up into his eyes and saw he meant business. But the hardness slowly disappeared.

She cleared her throat and tugged her hand back. The questions she'd been asking herself about this man were answered in that brief collision of gazes. Was she ready to allow a man into her life again?

"I better get going." Ryan stood quickly, whisking the sketch off the table.

"Yes. You have a murderer to catch." She couldn't look him in the face. This revelation would take some getting used to.

Shandra followed him to the front door.

Ryan stopped with his hand on the door knob. "I may have more questions for you. Would you be able to come down to town...I-we could meet for a meal or something."

"We'll see what you drag up that you have to question me about." She wasn't committing to anything where this man was concerned.

"Okay. Thanks." He held up the sketch and opened the door, disappearing as he shut it behind him.

"Ella, what is going on?" Shandra leaned against the door. This was the first man since her art instructor at college to make her insides quiver and her heart race. "But look where that got you."

~*~

Ryan didn't use the siren or race off the mountain. He had a lot to think about and not just the case. Shandra Higheagle was getting under his skin. In a good way. But he'd read something in her eyes. She'd been hurt before. Would Naomi Norton know what or who had hurt Shandra? He shook his head. It would be unprofessional to ask a suspect about a witness. But once this case was closed and whether Naomi was the killer or not, he'd ask her questions about Shandra. He could tell from the battle Shandra fought within herself that it would take a while before she was comfortable telling him about her past. As touchy as she was about her ancestry, he'd bet his '57' Chevy it had to do with that.

He drove through town and straight to the resort. Rather than waste time walking from the parking lot that sat off to the side of the lodge, he parked right in front.

The valet started to say something, but Ryan flashed his badge and kept on walking. Inside he strode to the registration desk.

"Hello. I'm Detective Greer with the Sheriff's office." He held out the sketch. "Is this person staying here?"

The older woman behind the counter stared at the drawing for a long time. "I haven't seen anyone who looks like this. Wish I had, he's a looker." She glanced up and smiled. "You aren't half bad yourself."

Ryan smiled back, not because he was vain but the woman appeared open to dialog. "What is your shift?"

"Seven to three."

"So you would only have seen this man if he checked in during the day. Could I get the name of the person who works the evening shift at the desk?" He slid his card across the counter.

"Now that would be sending you to a much prettier and younger woman." The plump woman with graying brown hair, gave him a suggestive come-hither tilt of her head.

"I assure you I'm only interested in finding this man."

Her bright red lips pouted, and she wrote a name and phone number on a piece of paper. "If you come back about two-thirty you can wait for her to come on shift."

Ryan laughed. "I'll give her a call. Who knows, I may be back."

With that parting shot, he left the clerk smiling and waving.

He called the number she'd given him and left a message.

An hour later, Ryan sat at a computer in the Huckleberry P.D. checking the pasts of both Sidney and Paula Doring. He had his sister in the Sheriff's department running financials on the pair. If the payments weren't coming from Sidney, he had to find out where they were coming from. He also had Blane out picking up Juan Lida for questioning. He had more he wanted to find out from the man.

Paula was from Seattle. Why did that city stick in his memory? Ryan flipped through the notes in his pad and stabbed the pen down on the word Seattle. Naomi Norton had visited her sister in Seattle.

He picked up the desk phone and dialed the sheriff's office in King County, Washington. After repeating his badge number, county, and a wish to speak with a detective more times than when he'd put a call through to the Pentagon several years ago, he finally had the person he wanted.

"Yes. I'm working a homicide case in Idaho and I was wondering if you could give me information on Paula Doring and Joyce Carter?" He waited as the sound of typing filled the empty space.

The tapping stopped. "Do you have some kind of ID I can use to make sure I get the right persons of interest?"

"Yes." Ryan rattled off both woman's socials and in

Paula's case her maiden name.

The click of a keyboard and then a throat cleared. "Got it. Where do you want me to send the information?"

"Huckleberry, Idaho P.D."

"Really?" The detective's deep voice rose an octave. "Isn't that where there's a ski resort?"

"Yes."

The man lowered his voice. "How about shipping me some info about the resort. My wife's been bugging me to take her somewhere."

"I'll send it out tomorrow, Detective Timens."

"Thanks. Your information should be to you by this afternoon. Looks like I'll be doing a lot of scanning."

The phone clicked and a dial tone hummed in Ryan's ear. He placed the receiver on the phone. "That must be some file on Joyce." He remembered her sister saying Joyce had been heavy into drugs and not of her own doing. How many times had she been caught?

Blane entered the building, shoving a red faced, cursing Juan Lida.

"Where do you want him?" Blane asked.

"Whoa, I asked you to bring him in for questioning not treat him like a gang member." The minute the words slipped out he regretted saying them. The precinct he'd worked out of in Chicago had an off-the-books directive to rough up the gang members to show them who was boss. It was following that directive and then offering to help a gang member that put him in the crosshairs of three rival gangs.

Blane stared at him.

"Just bring us both a cup of coffee, please." Ryan motioned for Lida to enter an empty room just off the main office. "I'm sorry. Officer Blane is new, young, and gets carried away with his tough cop act."

His pleasant tone seemed to appease the man. Lida nodded and took a seat at the table in the middle of the room.

Blane entered with two cups of coffee in Styrofoam cups. Ryan hated drinking from Styrofoam. He put the cup down and thanked Blane, nodding for the young officer to leave. When the door closed, Ryan leaned back in his chair.

"I had a couple more things I wanted to ask you last night."

Lida took a sip of coffee and winced.

"Yeah, they make a piss poor cup of coffee here." Ryan pulled out his notepad and flipped to a clean page. "I understand from a third party that you made the statement you and Mrs, Doring were to be married."

"Sí. Yes. When her divorce from that womanizing man was final, we were to be married and become partners in the gallery."

The man's native accent was more prominent today. His fingers moved in a wave-like motion on the coffee cup. It appeared this questioning made the man nervous.

"Who else knew of these plans?"

His eyes narrowed then flicked wide as if in innocence. "No one. We were keeping it quiet to not give her husband a chance to take the gallery away from her."

Ryan peered steady at the man. He didn't show any tics of a liar. If Doring was giving his wife money once a month for the gallery, that would stop with the divorce. Was she afraid he would pull it sooner if he learned of her marriage to the assistant? He dropped the money and moved to the point she'd had two clandestine meetings. She wasn't telling Lida everything and perhaps was stringing him along.

Ryan pulled the sketch out of the file he'd brought into the room with him. "Do you know this man?"

Lida's nostrils flared as he glared at the sketch. "No." He spit the word out with emphasis.

"But you've seen him before? Where?" Had Juan seen the man with his lover and killed the woman in a rage? It would fit with the strength it would take to force the blunt object through her rib cage.

"Yes. He and Paula were arguing one day when I arrived at the gallery. She told him to leave, and then refused to say more than he was a man from her past." Lida shoved the sketch across the table. "She was still upset later that day and sold an expensive piece of art for half the price it should have gone for."

"But you don't have any idea what his name is or how he was part of her past?" Lida wasn't a U.S. Citizen but that wouldn't keep him from finding a way to discover the man's identity.

"No."

The quick refusal and staring at the table said Lida was lying. But there wasn't much Ryan could do other than bluff and say they would deport him if he didn't fess up. However, Ryan wasn't the kind to bluff and not follow through. He didn't want to mess with the INS when he had a murder to solve.

"If you discover who this man is please contact me." Ryan slid his business card across the table. "I have reason to believe he had something to do with Paula's death."

That caught the man's attention.

"What?"

"He was seen arguing with Mrs. Doring the day before her murder and possibly slipping into the back door of the gallery." Ryan knew he'd stretched the truth. If he believed Naomi Norton's story, the man the victim was seen arguing with more than once could have been the person slipping into the unlocked back door.

Lida leaned forward his eyes wide. "By who?"

"The woman you gave a copy of the gallery key."

Lida's dark complexion lightened two shades.

"Were you in the habit of giving anyone who asked keys to your employer's gallery?" This time he was going to lay it on heavy. "How many other people had access to the gallery through the back door?"

Lida dropped his face into his hands. "I have killed *mi amor*."

Chapter Fifteen

*Shandra walked beside a stream following a pretty
butterfly as it flit up and down and in circles. The roar
of fast moving water caught her attention. The trickling
stream grew in size and the water overflowed the banks.
Shandra grabbed a tree branch and pulled herself up.
The water rose and buildings started floating by. Most
of them were Huckleberry businesses. How could that
be? She was up the mountain from the town? She
looked up into the sky. Her grandmother's face
appeared in the clouds. "Ella, what are you—?"*

*A shout drew her gaze back to the fast running
river. The man she'd sketched was on a raft with the
warrior bronze she'd witnessed in Paula's gallery. He
pulled the spearhead off the shaft and threw it at her.*

*The hard object struck her in the chest, knocking
her into the water. Panic encompassed her. She
swallowed water and felt her body sinking. No! I have*

*to find the truth. Frantic to get out of the water that carried her away from the mountain, she flailed with leaden arms and bobbed to the top. On the far side of the stream she saw a familiar figure. "Ryan! Ryan!"*

Shandra's eyelids opened. She stared into the darkness, gradually realizing she wasn't in water. Her soft bed was under her, but she couldn't breathe. A glance down her body found the answer. Sheba covered her. The animal's huge head inches from Shandra's face. She inhaled nasty dog breath and shoved on the dog.

"Off." Her hoarse voice caught her by surprise. She clutched her dry aching, throat.

In two beats of her heart the dream came back in vivid images. The bronze statue of a warrior with a spear was a clue. Ella was feeding her clues in her dreams. But how? Why?

She stared at the ceiling. "How do I get into the gallery and look at the statue?" It was risky to break in, but what choice did she have? "I can't say to Ryan, hey, I had a dream and I think you should look at the warrior in the gallery."

Shandra rolled over and slugged the pillow next to her. "Why am I having these dreams?" The moonlight cast a beam across the photo on her dresser of she and Ella taken the summer she spent at the reservation. "No, I am not full blood. I'm not a shaman." She had shoved the stories and grandmother's persistence that she, Shandra, had the gift of sight to the back of her mind. When she returned to life at the ranch in Montana her mother and stepfather told her those were all an old woman's stories and fantasies.

Peering at the photo, Shandra was wondering if

perhaps the old woman had seen something in her granddaughter that no one else could see, including herself. It was absurd to think she had any kind of sight. She, after all, had her mother's practical mind. And my father's adventurous nature. The trait her mother hated and squelched whenever she could.

~*~

Shandra was up with the sun once again. This time she sat on the porch sipping coffee and trying to figure out the best way to get into the gallery. She hadn't slept much after the dream. And now that the details were ingrained in her mind, she felt compelled to discover if the top of the spear would come off.

At eight she pulled out her cell phone, scrolled to Naomi's number, and pushed the button.

"Hello. You're calling early," Naomi responded.

"You don't know the half of it." While they had become good friends, she only told Naomi parts of her life.

"I'm sorry. Can I help?"

Just as she'd expected Naomi, the giver, offered to help. She'd give the shirt off her back even if it was her last one. Precisely why Shandra knew her friend didn't kill Paula.

"Do you still have the key to the Doring Gallery back door?"

"I do, but…Why do you want to go in there?" Naomi whispered.

"I want to look around." She was practical enough to not tell her friend about the dream.

"That's the job of the police."

*Wow*. She hadn't expected Naomi to disagree.

"I plan to call the police if I find what I think I will.

But it seems senseless to call until I have the facts."

"What facts? What have you been doing?" The curiosity in her voice proved she'd give in.

"I made a sketch yesterday of the man Lil saw arguing with Paula."

"Who is he?"

"I don't know." She'd thought given the camaraderie she'd felt with Ryan, he would have at least called and let her know the man's name when he found out.

"Is he why you need to get into the gallery? Do you think he was one of Paula's artists?"

*That works!* "Yes. I know she keeps flyers of the artists. I want to slip in and see if I can find him."

"Come to the gallery, and I'll give you the key." A hand muffled the sounds on Naomi's end. "But don't tell Ted why you're here," she whispered and hung up.

A headache started to pound at her temples. Shandra went into the house and took two pain relievers. It's from lack of sleep, she told herself and not that she was about to do something illegal.

~*~

Ryan slept on the couch in the break room at the police station. The King County detective hadn't been exaggerating that he had a lot of information to scan. Ryan read through sixty-three scanned pages of information and crashed on the couch when his eyes gave out.

Between all of Joyce's arrests and Paula's they could have filled a court docket for a year. They were both arrested multiple times for drug offenses. The older woman's records were a decade before Joyce's. Paula started in her teens where Joyce didn't show up in the court records until she was in her mid-twenties. By the time Joyce was making court appearances it seemed Paula had cleaned up and moved on to the more lucrative trade of high-end prostitution. That was until she landed Sidney Doring, a philanthropist who must not have done a thorough background check on his new wife.

Blane arrived whistling and carrying a box of donuts. The scent of the yeasty cholesterol-laden treats made Ryan's stomach rumble. He'd skipped dinner last night and on his empty stomach didn't dare try to drink the acid the Huckleberry P.D. called coffee.

"You want a donut? They're fresh." Blane opened the lid and flashed him with chocolate and maple covered bars and glazed donuts, wafting the scent into Ryan's face.

"I need real food. Don't mess up the pile of papers in the interrogation room. I'll be back." Ryan buckled on his shoulder holster.

"You slept here last night?" Blane's gaze swept the room.

The blanket Ryan had used draped over the back of the couch and the pillow still had an indentation from his head.

"Seemed senseless to pay for a motel when I didn't get to sleep until two." He shoved his Glock in the holster and pulled a long sleeved denim shirt on, leaving it unbuttoned over a gray t-shirt. "I'll be back in an hour."

Walking would do him good after sleeping on the small couch. The town was quiet as he ambled up Second Street to the restaurant two blocks down from the crime scene. He'd had breakfast here yesterday and liked the price and the amount of food.

He stepped inside and scanned the establishment. Treat, the funeral home driver, waved at him. The man knew a lot about Joyce Carter. Did he know about Paula's past as well? Ryan crossed to the counter and took a stool next to Treat.

"Detective, you came to the right place to get a good meal." Treat smiled at the African American woman in her mid-thirties smiling back at him from the kitchen window.

"I was here yesterday and enjoyed the meal." Ryan looked from the woman to the man and back to the woman. "You two look like you know one another well."

"That there's Ruthie, my soon-to-be wife." Treat winked and the woman giggled.

"Congratulations!" Ryan slapped Treat on his back and found what he expected. Solid muscle.

"You got a woman, detective?"

A high school-aged girl poured Ryan a cup of coffee and handed him the menu. He glanced at Treat's plate. "Just give me what he's having."

The girl grinned, scribbled on the pad, and placed it in line with the other orders.

He took a sip of the coffee and closed his eyes. Nothing beat a good cup of coffee.

"Best coffee in town." Treat said. "You got a woman?"

"No, not at the moment." Shandra's face came into his mind and he smiled.

"But you're thinking about one." Treat bumped Ryan with his elbow.

"Yeah. That's what men do. Think about what it

feels like to hold a woman." He was fishing with that comment. He'd only met Treat the one other time. The man had seemed to know a lot and have some scruples but that could have been a front for a police officer.

Treat's lips turned into an even bigger grin as he stared heatedly at the cook. "Only if it's the right woman." He turned his gaze on Ryan. "There are men in this town that hold anything that doesn't have testosterone, but they are missin' out on the communion of two souls."

Ryan nodded his head. That's why he hadn't married. He'd yet to find that person who made him feel whole. The waitress set Ryan's plate in front of him. He smiled and peered into Treat's eyes.

"I have some questions for you." He glanced briefly toward the kitchen, then the young waitress, and nodded toward an empty booth in the back of the room. Ryan picked up his plate carrying it to the booth. Treat followed, carrying his breakfast and coffee.

Treat slid into the seat and leaned forward over his plate. "What's this about?"

"You seemed to be well versed in Joyce Carter the day we met. I have some questions about her and her sister."

"Naomi? You don't think she killed Paula do you?" The incredulous tone said he would champion the woman just like Shandra.

"There has been some evidence that points to her." Ryan held up a hand when the man leaned back his face darkening in anger. "But I have to uncover everything to find the killer. What do you know about Joyce's life before she came here?"

"Not more than I said before. Her old boyfriend got

her hooked on drugs, and she went into rehab as soon as he went to jail." The disgust in his voice paralleled Ryan's thoughts about the ex-boyfriend.

"Tell me about Joyce. Was she as timid and fretful as her sister? I can't see a strong-willed woman getting hooked on drugs if she didn't want to."

"Joyce was sweet, soft spoken, had a body that men drooled over and even though she'd been in the drug scene was as naïve as a school girl." Treat chewed a bite of his hash browns a thoughtful repose on his face. "I could see her trying to please a man she thought cared for her." He wielded his fork like a pointer. "I only visited with her at length a couple times. Once when she came to the funeral home looking for a job, and then one day here in the diner."

The man's expression changed as he thought back. "You know. She was jumpy the time I talked with her here. I asked her what was wrong. She just said, you can't run from your past."

Ryan latched onto that piece. "So you think her past arrived in Huckleberry?

Treat shook his head. "I don't think it was a person." He raised his coffee cup, and the teenaged waitress promptly arrived, refilling his cup and Ryan's.

"Do you know if she made any friends here? Anyone she may have confided in besides her sister?" Ryan wondered if the photos Paula had were the reason Joyce thought her past had caught up to her."

"I only saw her alone or with Ted and Naomi." Treat stopped eating. "Ruthie, come out here a minute," he called.

The cook smiled, waved a flapjack turner, and turned to the young man in a chef's hat. A couple minutes later she arrived at the booth a cup of coffee in one hand. She slid in beside Treat.

"Ruthie, this is Detective Greer. He's trying to find out who killed Paula."

Ryan held his hand out over the table. The woman had a firm grip and a ready smile.

"You got any suspects?" she asked and took a sip of coffee.

"A couple. You have any ideas?" The woman worked in what looked to be the hangout of the local business people. Ryan hoped she was one who listened in on conversations.

"Paula had a lot of lunch meetings where she'd come in, pick up food for two, and leave."

Ryan pulled out his notepad. "Any thoughts on who she was seeing?"

Ruthie laughed. "Half the male artists in her gallery. Half the business men in town. That woman needed a lesson in keeping her knees together."

Ryan glanced up from his notepad. *Could the extra money each month have been from prostitution? Had her husband found out?* "Did she get paid for keeping company with these men?"

Treat and Ruthie looked at one another, then back at him.

"I never wondered about that. I just figured she was one of them women that had to have it all the time and Doring couldn't take care of her." A lop-sided grin gave the impression Treat found it humorous Doring couldn't provide what his wife needed.

Ruthie slapped Treat's arm. "That's not a nice thing to say about Mr. Doring. And I know he didn't have any problem with that."

"How so?" Ryan turned his attention to the woman.

"Yeah, how'd you know that?" The accusation in Treat's voice didn't seem to bother the woman. She just patted his beefy arm and smiled sweetly.

"A couple of the female employees at the lodge were in here one day and nearly got in a cat fight when they realized they'd both been sleeping with Doring." Ruthie sat back in the booth looking smug.

"Ruthie!" The young man in the kitchen called in a panic.

Her gaze whipped to the kitchen window and she stood. "Gotta go. Kyle's in training, and I don't need my kitchen burned down."

Ryan stopped her. "Do you know those two women's names?"

Ruthie shook her head and hurried to the kitchen.

Looked like he'd be making another trip to the lodge today.

"I gotta go too. My pop doesn't like me to be late." Treat tossed money on the tables. "See ya later babe!" he called out to the kitchen and left.

Ryan took a moment to prioritize the leads he needed to follow. 1. Show the sketch Shandra made to staff at the motels between town and the lodge. 2. Check Juan Lida's alibi for the time of the murder. 3. Check Sidney Doring's alibi for the time of the murder. 4. See where Joyce and Paula's lives might have intersected before Huckleberry.

He put money on the table and left the restaurant. Peering down the street he spotted Shandra's Jeep in front of Dimension Gallery. The thought of talking with the woman put a bounce in his step and a smile on his lips.

He continued down the sidewalk toward the Jeep. At the vehicle, he did a cursory check of the interior and turned to the gallery. Through the front and side windows in the building, he caught a glimpse of Shandra crossing the street toward Doring Gallery.

Instead of entering Dimensions, he strode around the corner just as Shandra walked into the alley behind the Doring Gallery. *What is she doing?*

Ryan jogged across the street and into the alley. Shandra wasn't anywhere in sight. The back door of Doring Gallery swung shut.

Chapter Sixteen

Shandra stopped inside the back door of the gallery and pulled a flashlight out of her purse. The LED beam shed a pristine white glow on the back room full of crates, packing material, and shadows. She'd never been in the backroom of Paula's gallery. The woman had always conducted all business at her office. Ted and Naomi welcomed artists to bring their pieces in through the back door and uncrate them. And when necessary, put them together.

Careful not to touch anything, Shandra proceeded through the room and into the back of the gallery. She hurried past the office. The door was closed, however her memory of what she'd found in there still haunted her. The air around her moved. A faint click echoed in the stillness. She stopped sweeping the light back and forth looking for the Native American display.

What made that click?

She listened, holding her breath. Nothing. *Nerves settle down. There's no one else here.*

Ahead of her the beam of light landed on the statue she trespassed to examine. Shandra tucked the flashlight between her knees, tugged a pair of rubber kitchen gloves from her back pocket and pulled them on. She had a box of the gloves in her studio to keep her fingers from drying out while working with the clay.

With the flashlight in her hand, she approached the statue with the spear. The artist did a magnificent job showing the abdominal muscles and the long lean muscles on the warrior's legs and arms. She ran a hand over the six-pack abs before moving up the arm and reaching for the spear.

The overhead lights flashed on, blinding her momentarily. Panic swelled her throat and raced her heart. Who caught her slinking around in the dark?

"What are you doing?"

She knew that voice. Had heard the same disappointment dripping from each word before. Shandra swallowed the lump, flicked off the flashlight, and slowly pivoted. Yep, it was the detective. The disbelief and disappointment on Ryan's face spun a web of guilt in her chest.

"I don't often misread people. Did you come back to find the murder weapon you hid?"

"No!" Anger shoved away the guilt of breaking in. She raised the flashlight, pointing it at his chest. "I did not kill Paula, and I am here looking for the weapon. But not because I used it."

He crossed his arms and stared at her. "Lady, your unjustified indignation isn't going to move me this time. I caught you trespassing on a crime scene."

"Yes, I'm trespassing. I didn't…" What was she supposed to say? My grandmother came to me in a dream last night and showed me the weapon. She laughed at the absurdity of the whole thing. She didn't believe in "visions" and here she was trespassing to seek information that came to her in a dream. The ludicrousness of her actions slapped her like a wet mop. *What was I thinking?*

Ryan's face grew tense, and his ears brightened to a deep red. "This isn't something to laugh about. Turn around." He pulled hand cuffs from behind his back.

That sobered her. "No! I'm not a criminal, and I didn't kill Paula."

"I don't want to get rough with you, but you're resisting arrest."

Ignoring him, Shandra flicked her flashlight back on and settled the beam on the tip of the spear. "I have reason to believe this is your murder weapon."

"Why?" The skepticism in his voice was better than the disappointment she'd witnessed earlier.

"It's awkward to tell you why. Since we're here could you just take a look?" She peered over her shoulder at Ryan. His arms were crossed again, and his chin jutted out in a stubborn set.

"I'd rather you explain your reasoning behind this." His gaze went to the four foot high warrior and then to the tip another foot above the warrior's head. "No one could pick that statue up and use it as a weapon. It's too heavy."

Exasperated, she grasped the shaft of the spear. "Not all bronzes are in one piece. This comes off." She tugged and nothing happened. Heat slithered up her neck, infusing her cheeks and ears.

"How?"

She shot a glare over her shoulder. "I don't know, but it does." Shandra twisted the shaft and it moved. Elation rushed through her like adrenaline. She spun the shaft faster and it rose.

"What the?" Ryan stepped beside her. "Let me take that." He spun the shaft three more times and it came loose. "How did you know that would come off?" His eyes narrowed, watching her.

"I-I…" She stared at her boots. Did she dare tell him the truth?

"Decide if you're going to tell me the truth while I call the station and have someone bring over my forensic kit." Ryan walked ten feet away and pulled his phone out of a holster on his belt.

He remained facing Shandra, his gaze leveled on her as he spoke into the phone giving orders.

How could she tell him what brought her here when she barely believed it herself? *You believed it enough to borrow a stolen key.* "Shut up."

"What?"

Mortification engulfed Shandra, making her cough and scorch with embarrassment. "I-I didn't mean you." How did she get out of this? "I was talking to myself."

Ryan's eyebrow shot up, and he shoved his phone in his phone holster as he strode toward her. "You won't get out of this on a mental plea."

*I must be crazy. Why else would I have believed a dream?* Shandra shook her head. "You'll never believe how I knew that could be the murder weapon." She held out her hands. "You might as well cuff me and take me to the station."

His dark eyes bore into her. The stare softened the

small amount of bravado she had left.

"You might tell me why you suspect this is the murder weapon rather than take the fall for someone else." Animosity no longer tinged his words.

She shook her head. "You'll never believe my story."

He tucked the hand cuffs away and placed the spear on the base of the bronze warrior. "Try me."

Shandra inhaled deeply and peered into his eyes. "This is crazy. I'm not even sure why I felt compelled to come here." She waved her hands stalling as her stomach gurgled with apprehension.

"But you did. Why?"

"I had a dream."

His brow wrinkled and his eyes narrowed. "What do you mean a dream?"

"Last night. I dreamed there was a flood. Ella, my father's mother who left this earth was in the dream."

His gaze zeroed in on her eyes. "Is this your Native American grandmother?"

"Y-yes. Why?" How did he know? Why was he so interested?

"What did she say?"

His interest unnerved her as much as telling him the dream that had brought her here. "She didn't say anything. In the dream she appeared when there was the flood. Then the man I sketched was on a raft and threw this spear at me, knocking me out of the tree I was in. I fell in the water and—" There was no way she would tell him he was there to save her.

"What?"

"I woke up with the need to come check out this bronze." Saying it out loud made it sound even more stupid than actually following through.

"So you think your grandmother is helping you solve the murder? Why?" His tone wasn't snotty or superior. His gaze searched her face.

"I don't know. Years ago she tried to tell me I had the gift of sight." Shandra clamped her jaws shut. That was more information than she'd planned to share with anyone, ever.

He continued to watch her. "You don't believe what your grandmother told you, and you can't believe you came here."

"It doesn't make sense, but I'm open to all options to prove Naomi didn't kill Paula and to expose whoever did."

The back door banged open. "Detective Greer?" Officer Blane hollered.

"Come to the front!" Ryan called then returned his gaze on Shandra. "Don't say anything. Let me do all the talking." He pointed at her gloved hands. "Get rid of those."

Shandra stripped the gloves off and shoved them in her back pocket.

Ryan leaned close, plucked the gloves from her pocket, and said, "We'll discuss your grandmother later."

Shandra stared at Ryan as he greeted Officer Blane. He seemed to take her dream and reason for coming here more seriously than she did. Warmth swirled in her chest. He believed her and in her dream. Her cheeks flushed reliving the feel of the heat of his fingers as he pulled her gloves from her back pocket.

Ryan couldn't help but smile at the confused expression on Shandra's face. He'd deal with her later.

Right now he had to get rid of Blane.

"Thank you for being so prompt." Ryan took his pack from Blane.

"What's she doing here?" Blane asked, glaring at Shandra.

"She was telling me about this statue and it made me wonder if this could be the murder weapon." Ryan nodded toward the spearhead as he shoved his hands into latex gloves and pulled out the luminol spray. He glanced at Shandra. Her attention was trained on the spray bottle in his hand.

He spritzed the bronze spear, held a black light flashlight above the spear, and waited. Gradually, blue appeared on the point and down to the broader part of the spear. It wasn't conclusive, but he'd bet the coroner would match the injuries in the body to this weapon as well as the victim's blood.

"What did she tell you that made you suspect that?" Blane nodded his head toward Shandra.

Blane's comment lit Ryan's anger like a match striking on metal. "Ms. Higheagle mentioned the spear could be removed."

Blane put his hand on his revolver. "How'd she know that?"

"Just because I am a potter doesn't mean I don't know how other pieces of art are put together."

Her haughty tone and the way she drew her body up straight and tall and peered down at the younger man, tickled Ryan and made the officer back away from her.

"I'll call dispatch and have a deputy retrieve this to take to the coroner in Coeur d'Alene." Ryan meant for his comment to send Blane on his way, but he continued to watch Shandra.

"Blane, you can go back to your duties, now." Ryan pulled out an evidence bag and placed the spearhead in the bag.

"Don't you think I should stay here until the deputy arrives?" Blane inched his hand toward his weapon.

"I'll be leaving here as soon as I finish testing the statue for prints and other signs of blood." Ryan wrote the time and date on the evidence bag and placed it in his pack.

"What about her? You want me to take her to the station?" Blane's tone didn't sound like he wanted to deal with Shandra. Which was fine with Ryan because he didn't plan to let her loose until they'd discussed her dream and why she didn't take it serious.

"I'll take care of Ms. Higheagle. You go back to work." When Blane didn't move, Ryan added, "That's an order. Get going or I'll call your chief."

The officer headed to the back door.

Shandra let out a long breath. "He doesn't like me. Reminds me of the Indian haters back in Montana." She shivered.

He wanted to comfort her, but he had work to do. "I don't think it's who or what you are, but more he came upon you at the murder scene and you're still a suspect in his mind."

"I guess so. Now what?" She watched him dust for prints on the statue and label them.

"I'd prefer you stay with me until I hand this over to a detective. Then I plan to have a discussion with you."

"About?" There was a quiver in her voice.

"Things." Ryan retrieved his phone and pressed

dispatch. His sister answered. "Cathleen, send a deputy to Huckleberry. I have evidence to go to Coeur d'Alene and forensics."

"You aren't taking it yourself? Bridget is going to be sad."

"She'll get over it. I have more important things to take care of here." He glanced at Shandra pretending to not listen in. "What's the ETA on a deputy getting here?"

"Thirty minutes."

"That works. Have them go to the P.D." He planned to drop off the evidence at the station, and then find a quiet place to talk with Shandra.

"Will do. Take care."

Ryan tapped the end button and faced Shandra. "Who would know that piece wasn't permanent?"

Shandra peered at him. "The artist, the foundry that poured the bronze, probably Paula, given the way she lorded over the artists and only let a few into the back room." She tapped a slender finger against her lips. "Probably Juan. That is if he was here when the bronze arrived and helped with the set up."

Ryan read the name of the artist on the base of the statue. *Oscar Rowan*. He pulled out his notepad. "Do you know this Oscar guy? Is he local?"

She shook her head. "I don't believe I've ever met him, which would lead me to believe he isn't local. The local artists gather about every three or four months and discuss ways to market and promote, not only here, but at other venues."

He stashed all the evidence in his pack and motioned for Shandra to head to the back of the building. "Since you have the key, we'll lock up on our way out." He glanced her direction and was pleased to see she cringed and blushed. It was a good telltale that she wasn't prone to trespassing. He hadn't thought she was, but when he'd watched her enter the building and then make her way straight for that bronze, his head and gut battled. He'd actually become physically ill thinking he'd misjudged another person. Especially Shandra.

He flipped off the lights. The LED beam of Shandra's flashlight guided them through the cluttered back room and straight to the door.

Once outside, he held out his hand. She dropped the key in his palm without hesitation. He locked the door and pocketed the key. He already had Lida's key, but had yet to discover if any more keys were floating around.

Shandra stood in the alley, her arms crossed, waiting.

"Why don't you walk with me over to the station? We'll grab a cup of coffee somewhere after I drop this off." He shouldered the pack and started down the alley. Her boot heels rang out on the pavement beside him as she strode forcefully down the alley.

Chapter Seventeen

Shandra didn't want to talk about her dream or her grandmother with Ryan, but she didn't see that she had much choice. If she begged off the conversation, she was pretty sure he would use the law, and the fact she was trespassing, to detain her. She'd rather not have the threat overshadowing their conversation.

Thankfully, Ryan didn't ask questions. The quiet as they walked to the police station gave Shandra time to rationalize her actions. She gathered logical reasons for her actions but always came back to reprimanding herself for following the dream. If she'd just written it off as a dream and went on with her day, she wouldn't be in this mess. For all she knew the spearhead being attached like that was a coincidence. The blood could have come from someone who worked on the statue. They'd come up with nothing, and she'd look even more guilty for throwing suspicion on a fake clue.

Ryan held the door to the Huckleberry police station open, waiting for her to enter. *At least I'm not in handcuffs.* She entered and immediately felt the stare of Officer Blane. There was another man she didn't know standing by an office door and an older woman sat at a desk behind a half wall.

"Have a seat. I'll only be a minute." Ryan pointed to a hard chair to the right of the entrance.

She nodded and sat, when she really wanted to turn and bolt out the door. The one other time she'd been inside a police station her stepfather had to bail her out. She and some friends had gone joy riding in Miriam's dad's new convertible. Someone had brought along a bottle of whiskey. They'd all tried it and during the reverie ran off the road. Unfortunately, it had been a county deputy who found them before they could contact a brother to come pull them out.

The look on her stepfather's face when he heard the circumstances had solidified her thoughts. *He only tolerates me for my mother's sake.* Adam Malcom had let it be known on more than one occasion that no one was to know she had Indian blood in her. Her mother said it was to protect her, but as Shandra aged, she discovered it was because her stepfather had a dislike for Native Americans. She never did find out the why, but did her best to get away from him as fast as she could.

"Hey?"

Shandra peered up into Ryan's concerned face. "What?"

"I said, I'm ready to go get that cup of coffee with you." His tone was soft, forgiving.

"Sorry, I was lost in thought."

He held the door open and she stood. "Anything you care to share?"

"No. You're not learning all my sordid secrets in one day." She managed a smile but didn't feel like smiling. She'd only told her mom, once, what Ryan was expecting her to spill. Mainly because if she kept denying it, she didn't have to come to terms with her heritage. Something she'd long ago decided didn't matter.

Out on the sidewalk, Ryan stopped. "Which way to the quietest coffee shop?"

"Unless you have a need for coffee, I'd rather go to the school grounds. Less chance of someone overhearing." Her stomach lurched. *Are you really going to tell him your grandmother believed you had sight?*

Ryan waved a hand. "Lead the way."

She'd hoped for a few more minutes to collect her thoughts, but he started in asking questions.

"What tribe are you?"

"Nez Perce."

"Idaho or Washington?"

Shandra stopped and studied the earnestness of his gaze. "Originally Oregon. My father's family is descended from the Wallowas and live on the Colville reservation."

He motioned for her to keep walking. "How did you end up in Montana?"

They entered the school grounds, and Shandra walked to the swings. She sat in a swing, pushing it back and forth with the toe of her boot dug into the sand. "My mother married my father when they graduated from high school. She was a barrel racer; he was a bronc rider. Only my mother was Caucasian and my father Indian. Even in the twenty-first century there was animosity toward the Native American. My parents had a rough time of it when they tried to settle down. But on the rodeo circuit, my father was revered for his riding skill. This is according to my grandmother. My mother won't talk about that part of her life with me."

"Why did your mother marry your father?"

"I've contemplated that many times over the years." This was a puzzle she'd been trying to piece together since she was old enough to understand love and marriage. "I received a huge inheritance from my maternal grandmother when she died, instead of my mother." She'd asked her mother why, but her mother refused to give a reason for her mother cutting her out of the will. "I believe my mother's rebellion put her at odds with her parents and possibly drove her to marry my father. Then, too much pride to say she'd made a mistake." The bitterness she felt toward her mother always made her voice go up an octave. "Fate stepped in, and she became a widow after a rodeo accident killed my father. She quickly married a son of a wealthy cattle rancher in Montana and forgot all about the five years she lived as the wife of an Indian."

"That bitterness you have has to be hard to live with." He peered into her eyes.

Shandra shrugged. "It wasn't until I turned thirteen that I finally spent time with Ella, my father's mother. She'd tried to have me visit many times but my mother wouldn't have it. That summer my step-father planned a vacation for him and my mother. They were going to leave me home with the housekeeper. I packed up and went to my grandmother's. My mother didn't want me to know my roots or become 'one of them'." She snorted. "Like by keeping me away from my relatives, I'd never want to know about that side of my DNA."

"It sounds like your mother worried more about her status than what was best for her daughter."

His quiet tone and steady gaze eased the tension that had tightened Shandra's shoulders.

"Yeah, since graduating high school, I started spending more time with my father's family than with my mom. I could tell it makes both she and Adam, my stepfather, happy to have me out of their lives."

"You don't mean that."

Did she glimpse pity in his dark eyes? That shored up her spine and put her back on the defensive. "What do you know about growing up in a house where you are told to keep half your life a secret and are disciplined when you ask questions?"

He raised his hands. "I won't press that subject anymore. We came here so you could tell me how a dream led you to believe the spear on that statue is the murder weapon."

It felt like her heart jumped into her throat. She swallowed several times to shove the apprehension back down away from her windpipe so she could talk.

"The summer I stayed with my grandmother, she told me I carried her gift of sight. The ability to see the truth when others lie." She glanced up to see if Ryan had a smirk on his face. When he didn't, she unclenched her aching hands from around the swing chains and placed them in her lap. "When I went home, all excited and talking of my gift, mother and Adam, of course, told me grandmother was an old woman who made up stories to entertain herself and those around her." After listening to that long enough and growing older and wiser, I too, realized it was just Ella's way of making me feel special and giving me a sense of belonging."

Ryan shook his head. "You didn't believe your grandmother? What was her position in the tribe?"

His knowledge of Native American culture struck her anew. "She was one of the leaders of the Long House and had a Seven Drum ceremony at her funeral. She made sure I was invited to that."

"It sounds like your grandmother was respected and spiritual." Ryan raised an eyebrow. "And even though you shunned your heritage, she made sure you were brought into a private Nez Perce ceremony. I would say she had more than an old woman's desire to show you where you truly belonged."

"How can someone like you have such knowledge and conviction about this?" Shandra couldn't believe she was talking as if having sight was normal.

"Tell me why you had to check that spear and I'll answer you." He crossed his arms and leaned against the swing set pole, nonchalantly crossing his ankles.

"Is this some kind of cop double talk?" She glared at him, still not comfortable with revealing her compulsion to follow her dream.

"No, it's me trying to learn more about this sight you say you have and discovering a murderer."

She pushed off with her foot and swung back and forth slowly. "Have you used a psychic before?"

"Not me personally, but there was one old detective in Chicago that used one. I found the whole concept interesting. How the psychic could give solid information on one case and not another." He shifted, leaning his back against the post and edging closer to her. He grabbed the chain and stopped her movement. "Stop stalling."

Shandra stared up into his face. He didn't have disapproval dimming his gaze or animosity blotching his face. But she saw determination in his eyes and the set of his chin.

"I told you. I had a dream. Ella was in it, the man I sketched threw that spear at me. That gave me the notion it was the murder weapon." She stared at the toe of her cowboy boots. "You're not going to tell people why I thought it was important to the case are you?"

Ryan stared down at Shandra's dejected posture. He couldn't stop his hand as it reached out and cupped her chin. He tipped her face up. "Why do you find it so hard to believe you have a gift?"

Her eyes narrowed, and she pulled her chin from his grasp. "The only gift I have is making art from the earth."

He crouched in front of the swing, putting his face level with hers. "As strong as your heritage comes through in your art, I don't see how you can be so adamant about ignoring your dreams."

"How can you, a White, feel so strong about my dreams?"

Ryan knew she'd be asking this question. His interest was not only in Native American myths and shamans, it went into his own heritage. "My mom is Irish, through and through."

"Greer isn't very Irish." Her brow remained furrowed and her gaze confrontational.

"That's my dad's name. He is a mixture of all that made this country, including a pint of Native American blood. But Mom was straight from Ireland when Dad married her. My siblings names are; Conor, Cathleen, and Bridget. Mom gave us very Irish names and tells stories of the wee people and the mysteries of her homeland. I grew up believing in the very thing you are running from."

Her gaze softened. "You believe in leprechauns?"

"I'm not a fool to go looking for a pot of gold, but I believe in the possibility."

A deep throaty laugh filled his ears like a seductive ballad. Her eyes no longer held suspicion.

"That's better. Now tell me every detail in this dream so we can catch a murderer." It warmed his heart when she smiled and began retelling her dream, only this time she didn't give the abridged version.

"When I was being pulled down the river I saw you on the bank and called to you." Shandra's cheeks took on a deeper hue as she added the last tidbit.

Ryan smiled. "Think that might have been a hint to contact me instead of hunting down the murder weapon on your own?"

Her golden eyes took on a new shimmer as she peered into his eyes. "I believe Ella thinks we will discover the killer together."

Heat flashed through his body. He'd been drawn to Shandra from the start, but this sudden sultry look and talk of them working together, reinforced his desire to discover all he could about the woman.

"I believe the same thing. So from now on, you need to pick up the phone when you have a dream and call me. Together we'll decipher its meaning and decide what 'lawful' actions to take."

She had the decency to blush at his cryptic mention

of her breaking and entering a crime scene.

"When will you know if the blood on the spear is Paula's?"

Ryan unlocked his knees and raised to his full height. "We should know by tonight." He held out his hand. She placed her fingers in his palm. Tugging her to her feet, he started back toward the city's hub. She didn't pull her hand from his, a small triumph.

"I need to figure out who knew the spear was removable on that statue." He kept his pace to a stroll.

"The artist, Paula, and Juan are the first I can come up with that would have been in Huckleberry. The piece would have arrived packed in a crate and someone would have had to put it together. I assumed the reason Paula hired Juan was for his strength to help with uncrating larger pieces." Shandra stopped.

Ryan faced her. "What?"

"If the artist brought the piece himself, it could have been all together or he could have assembled it with only Paula knowing the spear was removable."

"So you're thinking the artist should be the first person I contact." Ryan resumed walking. His hand tugged out of Shandra's when she didn't continue. "Are you coming?"

"We can go back to the gallery and get the contact information for the artist from Paula's records." Shandra tipped her head as if she challenged him to return to the gallery.

"Let's head over there." When he reached out to reclaim her hand she avoided him by breezing by at a quick pace. Was she that excited to get to the crime scene or using the pace to avoid being seen holding his hand? He rubbed at the tension building in his neck.

She seemed to be the more professional of the two. It would be in bad taste for him to go strolling down the street holding the hand of the person who discovered the body and was still a suspect in some people's eyes.

Chapter Eighteen

Shandra had to put distance between she and Ryan. She was allowing him closer than anyone in her life. And her body was reacting to his presence in ways she'd only experienced once before and that encounter had driven her deeper into herself. She didn't like the person she'd been after that relationship.

Ryan tilted her view of things and tilted her common sense. The latter was just as scary as her body's reaction to him.

At the gallery, she stopped in front of the back door and waited for Ryan to retrieve the key from a pocket. He brushed past her and sent her body into a tither. *Get over this. He's no different than any other male I've encountered.* Deep down she knew he was much different than any other man she'd had in her life.

Ryan touched the door and it moved. He motioned for her to step to the side as he drew a gun out from under his denim shirt.

She stood outside the door for two breaths, then tiptoed quietly behind him as he advanced into the building. The sound of cursing and snapping came from inside the office. Had the murderer returned to the scene of the crime?

Ryan stopped and she thumped into his back. He spun, grabbing her with his empty hand. "I told you to stay outside?" he hissed into her ear.

"I thought you were just motioning for me to allow you to go first." She batted her eyelashes, knowing he couldn't see it in the dim light. But her voice had deepened to the sultry flirtatious tone she'd used on many occasions to get a male to do her bidding.

"Stay here." He whispered, giving her arm a quick squeeze.

Reluctantly, she stood her ground. But she searched the dim lighting and listened intently as Ryan crept toward the office.

The second he disappeared into the room, Shandra scurried forward.

"Hey! Let go of me!"

Shandra closed her eyes and listened. Why did that male voice sound familiar?

"What are you doing in here? This is a crime scene, no one is allowed past the yellow tape." Ryan's tone was laced with irritation.

"Paula owed me money. I figured since she won't be selling my stuff, I was coming to get it."

"In the office? Your art would be in the gallery. All artists have been contacted and told their work is part of the investigation. They, and you, will have to go through proper channels to get it back." Ryan had lost his patience with the person. It rang in his voice. "Turn around."

"What are you doing?" The voice rose in disbelief.

The click of handcuffs, she well remembered from her recent experience, revealed the man's fate.

"You're under arrest for breaking and entering and…Shandra, come in here, please."

Ryan didn't have to request twice. Shandra popped through the door and stopped in her tracks. She didn't know the man's name, but she'd noticed him at several of Paula's exhibits.

"Stop!" Ryan ordered as she started to walk toward the two. "Don't step on the pieces on the floor. See if you can find a plastic bag or something to put the pieces in. I'd like to take them with us."

Shandra scooted into the private restroom and found a box of sandwich bags. At her return, Ryan had the man sitting in a chair with his hands laced through the arms and cuffed.

"Yes, the gallery again. Bring my forensic bag. I have a suspect to be transferred to the station." Ryan shoved his phone back in the holster on his belt and knelt at the stick-looking pieces.

She handed him the box of bags.

"These will work." He put one on his hand like a fingerless glove and picked up the pieces placing them in another bag.

By the time all the pieces were gathered, Officer Blane came charging into the room.

"Take this man to the station, get his information, and hold him until I get there." Ryan glared at the handcuffed man.

Shandra glanced down at what appeared to be the

overturned base for the pieces Ryan had picked up. Writing scrawled across the bottom. *My love twines around you like a clinging vine, giving you nourishment.*

Officer Blane unlocked the cuffs and jerked the suspect to his feet.

"Hey!" the intruder glared at Officer Blane.

"Blane, take it easy, I want him cooperative when I get there to question him." Ryan's rebuff didn't seem to sink into the zealous young cop. He clicked the cuffs back on the man and pushed him out the door.

"One of these days that kid's going to do that to the wrong person and end up on his ass." Ryan shook his head.

"Look at this.' Shandra tugged on Ryan's shirt sleeve and pointed to the base and writing. "I'd say from that inscription, you may have another one of Paula's love interests."

Ryan unzipped the backpack Officer Blane left and donned a pair of latex gloves. He picked up the object and turned it around and around inspecting it.

A chuckle bubbled up Ryan's throat as he realized what he held.

"What?" Shandra asked, pushing closer and staring at the object in his hand.

Did he tell her this was a rather provocative scene of two bodies entwined in the act of love?

"I saw this in its entirety when I took photos of the crime scene."

"Really? Was it interesting?" She leaned closer, staring at the base as if she could see what it had been.

"You'll never guess what it was." Ryan slipped the base into one of his plastic evidence bags and wrote on it.

"Knowing Paula, it was probably evocative."

He stared at the women next to him. "What do you know about Paula's past?"

Her eyes widened and she peered into his. "Nothing. I was talking about the amount of men I've seen fawning all over her. She seemed to ooze something that drew the men to her." Shandra took a step back from him and crossed her arms. "I always thought she and Sidney made a fitting couple the way they cheated on each other." She narrowed her golden eyes giving the appearance of a wild cat zoning in on prey. "What is in her past?"

Ryan exhaled a huge sigh, releasing exasperation at himself for bringing up the subject with the woman staring him down like a pro. "I'm not at liberty to tell you."

Fisted hands jammed onto her hips. "Then you shouldn't drop interesting comments like that if you don't want me to dig deeper."

"I know. I'll censure myself from now on." He stuffed all the evidence in his bag and took several quick photos of the area. "Let's get the information we came for." He handed Shandra a pair of gloves. If for some reason they had to reprint something, he didn't want her prints to end up on things.

Ryan turned the computer on, waited for it to boot up and discovered that it required a password. "While I try to discover her password, you want to see if you can find any information about Oscar Rowan in her file cabinet?"

"Oscar Rowan…" Shandra repeated the name again. Her fingers snapped. "That's who he is?"

"What?" Ryan faced the woman. Her mind ran faster than a jackrabbit. "Who?"

"The guy you sent with Officer Blane is Oscar Rowan, the artist who made the statue." Her eyes sparkled, and her lips turned up at the corners in a conspiratorial smile.

This case was making less and less sense. "I thought you didn't know the artist?"

"The name didn't click until I heard his voice and saw his face. He was in an animated conversation with Paula at the last art council meeting setting up this weekend event."

"Why was he smashing a fragile piece of art when the murder weapon was on his statue?" Ryan dug his fingers into the knot forming at the base of his neck.

"You haven't confirmed that was the murder weapon."

Ryan stared at Shandra. How could she have so little faith in herself? He believed her dream revealed the weapon. Now, if she could just dream about the man in the sketch, they could have more to go on.

"We'll know for certain tonight." He motioned for her to head back to the door. Once he deposited her in her Jeep, he was heading to the police station and questioning Rowan. He wouldn't have anything concrete to ask him until the spear made it to Coeur d'Alene and the test proved it was Paula's blood in the crevices.

Chapter Nineteen

Shandra's mind wandered as she drove down Main Street to the gas station and Jiffy Mart. Elbert, the same elderly gentleman who manned the two gas pumps since she'd moved to Huckleberry, shuffled out of the store.

"Afternoon, Miss. Need it filled up?"

"Yes, please." She'd planned to stay in the vehicle until an idea struck. Shandra dug into her leather fringed bag and pulled out a copy of the sketch she'd given Ryan. She exited the Jeep and walked over to Elbert, who stood with one hand resting on the nozzle filling her car.

"Have you seen this man around here?"

Elbert grasped the paper in a gnarled hand and shoved his glasses tighter against his head with the other. "Don't think so. I can tell you he isn't a local. At least not one that comes to this gas station."

"He was seen behind the—" She stopped as his words registered. *There were two gas stations.* This one had a Jiffy Mart and the one, on the way to the lodge, had a Quik Mart. Lil had said Quik Mart. She'd been at the gas station on the other side of town.

Shandra impatiently waited for the tank to fill. When Elbert finally twisted the cap on and she handed him her debit card, he shuffled into the store with her on his heels. She had figured this was the gas station and Quik Mart Lil frequented because it was on the way to the mountain.

With her gas purchased, she slid behind the wheel of her Jeep and headed across town to the Quik Mart, taking Fir Street to drive by the police station. Ryan's Tahoe was parked in front of the building. She hoped that meant he was interrogating Oscar and not out showing the sketch around. If she ran into him, she was pretty sure he wouldn't think twice about detaining her for obstruction of something. Even though he had let her slip by with several of her indiscretions with this murder, his tolerance had to be getting thin.

At the Quik Mart station a young man jogged between four pumps. The location at the intersection of Highway 90 and the road to Huckleberry Lodge and Ski Resort made this the busier of the two stations.

Shandra parked the Jeep and walked inside. A woman with gray hair bobbed to her earlobes and a younger woman in her mid-twenties with tattoos, a nose stud, and magenta spiked hair stood behind the counter ringing up items and asking for pump numbers. Shandra stood in line, waiting her turn to speak to the older woman.

"What pump?" The clerk asked when it was

Shandra's turn.

"No gas. Have you seen this man?" She spread the sketch out on the counter in front of the woman.

"I already told you police, there are too many come through that door for me to remember them all." The clerk peered over Shandra's shoulder and scowled.

Shandra peeked behind her. There wasn't anyone in line so she persisted. "Look at that face. You can't tell me a woman wouldn't notice him."

The younger woman leaned over and stared at the paper.

"That man is a hunk. If he came in here I would have noticed him." The younger woman licked her lips and smiled. "Yeah, he would have been eye candy if he'd wandered in here."

"So you're saying you haven't seen him?" The man was like a ghost. "He was behind this store four days ago arguing with a woman."

The older woman perked up. "Arguing? I might have heard that quarrel. I was sitting just inside the back door on my break when a man and woman were going at it."

Shandra couldn't believe the woman would sit and listen and not peek. "You didn't look out to see who was arguing?"

"Oh, I knew who the woman was. You couldn't miss that attitude and shrieking voice. It was Paula Doring." The woman nodded, and her gray hair bounced around her face.

"You knew Paula Doring?" This was better than she'd expected.

"Sure. Her husband keeps an account with us. Pays monthly for their gas and anything else they purchase here." The woman waved Shandra to the side.

Shandra stepped over but didn't leave the counter. Once the customer left, she returned to her position directly in front of the woman. "What were the two arguing about?"

"Paula said his showing up was poor timing. He said, her husband asked him to visit."

"Why?" Shandra couldn't believe Sidney knew the person they were looking for. Had Ryan shown the sketch to him?

"I don't know. That's when they started arguing. All I heard was her shrieking. His voice was real low and hard." The woman shivered. "I couldn't hear his words but the way he was saying them they didn't sound none to friendly." Her eyes widened. "Did he kill Paula?"

"That's what we're trying to figure out. Thank you." Shandra folded the copy of the sketch and slid it into her sketch book in her purse and exited the building.

Ryan stood beside the gas attendant, the paper with her sketch in his hand. What would he say if he went in and found out she'd already asked a bunch of questions? But the woman had said the police had already been there. Why was Ryan back?

She sauntered up to the two. "Are you following me, detective?" she asked in as playful a tone as she could muster knowing she'd been encroaching on his business.

"Thank you," he said to the young man and faced her. "I found it odd that you were headed the opposite direction from your home as you drove by the police station."

"I needed gas."

"According to the attendant you didn't fill your Jeep. You were harassing the women inside." He raised an eyebrow as if waiting for her to come up with another lie.

Shandra threw up her hands. "Okay, when I realized that Lil meant this Quik Mart and not the Jiffy Mart as I'd thought, I came over here to see if anyone had seen the man in the sketch."

"Blane has already been here." Ryan crossed his arms and peered at her with his unemotional cop expression.

"Well, he didn't ask the right questions." She hid the smirk quirking her lips when he uncrossed his arms and took a step toward her.

"You found out something about the mystery man?"

"Buy me lunch and I'll spill everything I found out."

"You know I shouldn't reward you for butting into police business." He crossed his arms again, but the expression on his face had softened.

"Fine, then let me buy you lunch, and I'll still give you all I found out." Shandra walked toward her Jeep.

"Let's walk." Ryan put a hand on her elbow and turned her toward Huckleberry Street. "I've become partial to eating at Ruthie's."

She knew the restaurant he meant. It was only two blocks from the gas station. "I don't mind walking this time of year. But don't expect me to do this in January or February. I prefer the indoors in the winter time."

"I'll keep that in mind."

The way he said it made her think he locked the

information up in a place for safekeeping. And that he might just be around when wintertime came. After this investigation was over she was pretty sure she'd not see the detective again. Huckleberry was usually a very peaceful place.

Ryan waved to Ruthie who was still in the kitchen cooking as he and Shandra entered the restaurant. He'd been five feet from stepping into the interrogation room and questioning Oscar Rowan when he spotted Shandra heading toward the lodge and not home. He couldn't shake the feeling if he didn't keep an eye on her she was going to find trouble.

"Find a seat anywhere. You missed the lunch crowd so there's plenty of room," Ruthie said as she waved her waitress, who was eating a salad at the counter, to stay seated.

Ryan escorted Shandra to the booth in the corner farthest from the kitchen and the resting waitress.

"Shandra, you gonna have your usual?" Ruthie handed Ryan a menu.

"Yes, and the bill is on me." Shandra settled into the padded bench seat as if she planned to stay a while.

"I'll have an iced tea, cheese burger, fries, and salad." Ryan closed the menu and handed it to the cook.

She beamed down at him and nodded her head. "I'll have that up in no time." When Ruthie passed her waitress she spoke to her and went on into the kitchen.

"It appears you come here often." He'd become a bit of a regular himself since taking on this investigation.

"Best burgers and shakes in town." Shandra leaned forward. "No one at the Quik Mart saw our man, but the older clerk heard him arguing with Paula Doring out back on the day Lil said she saw the argument."

Ryan pulled out his notepad and pencil. "What did she hear?"

"Paula said something about poor timing for the man to show up. The man replied her husband called him."

Ryan glanced up from his notepad and stared at Shandra. "That was exactly what the woman heard?"

She bobbed her head. "She said after that Paula did a bunch of shrieking and the man's voice became threatening, but she couldn't hear what was being said."

Ryan slammed the notepad down on the table. "I showed that sketch all around the lodge and everyone said they'd never seen the man."

"Did you show it to Sidney?"

"He was released by the time I had the sketch, and he wasn't at the lodge when I was there. Or at least that's what I was told." Ryan flipped through his pages. "This bit of information gives me more to go after Doring with."

The waitress arrived with his tea and a large milk shake.

"Thank you, Rae Ann," Shandra said, pulling the paper off a straw and pushing it into the creamy drink in front of her. She drew on the straw and her eyes closed.

What he wouldn't give to see that contentment on her face after they'd spent a night together. He snatched back that thought. Those kinds of thoughts would only mess with his investigation and get him mixed up with a woman. He'd sworn off them until he determined if this was where he wanted to stay or if he would regroup here and then head back to the city.

He cleared his throat and his thoughts. "What flavor is that you're enjoying?"

"Caramel." She slid the malt glass that was now a quarter empty to the middle of the table. "Do you think Sidney killed Paula?"

"I can't see him getting his hands dirty that way, but I could see him paying someone to do it." Ryan tapped the pocket holding the sketch. "I'd really like to get my hands on this guy. If he was paid by Doring, I might be able to get him to roll."

"But how would he know about the statue coming apart?"

Her logic was attractive.

"He could have been in the gallery when the statue arrived and was uncrated. Lida saw him at the gallery arguing with Paula once." He was keeping a running tally of the suspects and so far few were getting marked off the list.

Chapter Twenty

Ryan sat across the interrogation table from Oscar Rowan. The man was twitchy as a meth user.

"What were you really doing in the office at Doring Gallery?"

Rowan picked at the edge of the vinyl table. "I needed money and figured I'd take back my art pieces."

"Why did you smash this?" Ryan pulled out a photo he'd taken of the entwined sticks on his initial investigation.

A shaky finger shoved the photo back at him. "That Mexican gave it to her. I saw the significance of the piece."

"What was the significance?" Ryan pushed the photo back to the middle of the table.

"That spic thought she'd marry him. She might have been sleeping with him, but she'd never marry a worthless shit like him." Rowan snorted and laughed.

"No, she didn't marry unless it meant money, and she didn't sleep with someone unless she planned to use them."

"It sounds like you knew the murder victim well. How is that?"

Rowan's eyes widened, and he stared at Ryan. "Got any water. My throat's dry."

Sweat popped out on his forehead, and his fingers started tapping on the table top. The man was a user. From Ryan's first observation he'd guess meth.

"Hold on." Ryan moved to the door opened it and waved his hand. Jolene the dispatcher hurried over. "Could you please bring a bottle or cup of water for my guest?"

"Yes, sir." The woman hurried over to the break room and returned with a paper cup of water.

"Thank you." Ryan took the cup and placed it in front of Rowan on the table. The man tossed it back like the elixir of life.

"Now, how well did you know Paula Doring?"

Rowan licked his lips drawing in the drops of water that remained. "We go back to when she was hooking in the Fremont District of Seattle. I was new to the art scene, and she had connections with every gallery owner and studio."

"You knew her before she married Doring?"

"Yeah. I couldn't believe it when she announced she was cleaning up and moving up in the world. Didn't see her for nearly a year. Then one night at a big art event here she comes strutting in on Doring's arm and flashing a big diamond ring." He smirked. "I had her that night before she went home with her soon-to-be-husband."

Hearing all about the murdered woman soured Ryan's stomach. While he had to find her killer, her lifestyle was less than favorable. He needed a change of subject.

"What made you think you could carry that huge statue of yours out of the gallery tonight?" Ryan studied the man. His eyes flicked back and forth as if his brain was scanning files to figure out what lie he'd told. Taking pity on him, Ryan helped. "You said you were in the gallery to get your pieces because Paula owed you money."

"Oh, right." Rowan wiped a shaky hand over his face. His legs started bouncing under the table. One was next to a table leg and made the furniture bounce.

Ryan moved the table to the right six inches. "What did you have in the gallery besides the warrior holding a spear?"

"I couldn't carry that. It weighs three-hundred-fifty pounds. I had a couple of smaller pieces I was going to take." The man smiled like he'd given a winning answer.

"Why were you in the office if you wanted to pick up your artwork?"

Rowan didn't meet his gaze. "I didn't know where they were in the gallery and was looking for paperwork to find them."

"It would have been faster to just walk around the gallery and pick them up."

Sweat glistened his forehead again. Rowan swiped at it with his shirt sleeve. "I guess I wasn't thinking clear."

"Could that be because you're on something?" Ryan leaned over the table toward the jittery suspect.

"Who uncrated your warrior and set it up in the gallery?"

"I don't know. The foundry sent it straight to Paula." He swiped a hand across his face again.

Ryan leaned back in his chair. The man was strung out on something. If he were the murderer why was he digging through the papers and things on the desk? It would have made more sense if he'd gone for the incriminating spearhead.

"You weren't at the gallery for your art. What were you really doing there?" Ryan flipped open a file Blane had put together on the artist after bringing him in. "It looks like you've been arrested for using several times. Did Paula have something on you?"

Rowan slapped his back against the chair, crossed his arms, and twitched. But his mouth remained firmly shut.

Ryan picked up the folder and walked to the door. Outside the room, he motioned to Blane who watched the interrogation room from a desk. "Put him in a cell until he's so dt'd he's ready to talk. Then go to the gallery and box up every piece of paper in that office. I want to know what he was looking for."

Blane nodded and marched into the interrogation room.

Ryan looked at his watch. It was about time he caught up with Doring and flashed the sketch at him.

~*~

Shandra arrived home and turned on the computer. She did an online search of Oscar Rowan, noting he was a relative new-comer to the large art scene, but had been building his art form in Seattle. There was very little about his past, where he went to school, or if he

152

had family. Just a photo of him and his creations which seemed to be stylistically different.

She typed in Sidney Doring. Multiple sites came up for him. He'd lived in Seattle before moving to Huckleberry. As a young man he was quite the partier. He used family money to buy his way into Huckleberry Lodge according to the Weippe County Chronicle.

Next, she typed in Paula Doring. The only information she could find on her was connected to the gallery and her marriage. How did someone marry a rich man and have no background?

Shandra glanced at her cell phone sitting on the desk in front of the computer monitor. Ryan knew Paula's past. He'd eluded to it earlier today and clammed up. What was in her past? Did it have anything to do with her death?

Clicking through the photo gallery of the Doring Gallery events, she paused on a photo of Paula and Oscar standing beside the warrior with the spear. Anyone checking out the photos would see the statue. But how would they know the spearhead came off? She clicked back to Oscar's website and scrolled to the section about the warrior. There it was. An inquisitive person could read this information and know the spearhead was taken off for packing.

That meant anyone who looked at this website could be a suspect. She popped a caramel in her mouth and sat back in her chair, staring at the computer screen. This investigation just went in circles. How did Ryan keep from going nuts when investigating something like this?

Shandra turned off the computer and went to bed. She had an order to finish tomorrow. As long as Ryan wasn't accusing Naomi of killing Paula, she had better things to do than try to play detective.

~*~

Ryan stood at the bar in the lodge. He'd learned through the registration clerk that Doring had been out of town but was expected to return this evening. Being the largest stockholder in the lodge, Doring had an apartment on the upper floor. The clerk had agreed to let Ryan know when the owner arrived.

He pivoted leaning his back against the bar and surveyed the nearly full room. For a week night the bar had a brisk business. Most of the people appeared to be guests of the lodge. Vacationers using the lodge as the base for day hikes and rafting excursions. He noticed one older couple who were at the art event. Flipping through the night in his mind, he remembered seeing Shandra speaking with the woman.

After scoping out the room, he started to turn back around when two people parted and he spotted a couple that surprised him. Picking up his iced tea, he sauntered across the room and stopped at the table.

"Mr. and Mrs. Norton, I didn't take you for the bar scene type." Ryan lowered himself onto a chair as Naomi's frightened gaze latched onto him. Ted cursed under his breath.

"We come here now and then to relax." Ted picked up what looked like whiskey on the rocks and took a sip.

Ryan tuned into the exhaustion in the man's voice. "This seems like a large crowd for a weeknight. Is it always like this?"

"We don't usually come here." Naomi blurted.

Ted shook his head and peered at his wife.

"I figured as much. You both look like cats with someone rocking on your tails. Want to let me know why you're here?" He leveled a stare at each one then leaned back in his chair when they only gave one another furtive glances. "I have a feeling we're waiting for the same person."

Naomi started to open her mouth, but Ted placed a hand on her arm, staying whatever had been about to spill out.

"Who are you waiting for?" Ted asked.

"Sidney Doring." Ryan kept his attention on the woman. She couldn't hide her emotions. Sure enough, she exhaled and fidgeted with the already shredded napkin in her hands.

"What makes you think we're waiting for Sidney?" The husband's calculated question didn't fool Ryan.

"Because you think he has answers about Joyce." Ryan hid the triumph he felt behind his standard blank cop expression. But watching the two peer at one another and shift in their seats validated his assumption. They thought because Paula had incriminating pictures of Joyce, the woman's husband would know something about Naomi's sister.

Taking pity on the two, he smiled. "Why don't you two go on home? I'll ask my questions and ask him about Joyce." He didn't want to let them know he already felt the two women were connected in some way other than just their addictions.

Naomi's eyes glistened with tears. "You'll tell us whatever you learn about her? Bad or good?"

As much as he wanted to keep Naomi Norton on his suspect list, her fragility didn't fit the strength or bravado it would take to plunge a blunt object like the spear through a rib cage.

"Yes. I'll tell you everything I learn about your sister." He'd printed out the files the King County detective sent him on the woman. When the Doring murder investigation was over, he'd give a copy to Naomi.

"Thank you." Naomi stood. "Come on Ted. I don't think my nerves can stand waiting any longer or asking the questions."

The relief that softened the etched lines on Ted's face proved he hadn't had the stomach to confront Doring either. Ryan was sure if he hadn't been here to deflect the two, Doring would have out-maneuvered and lorded over the couple.

Ryan watched the Nortons exit the bar. He followed behind, making sure they weren't pulling a fast one. They left the building and handed a ticket to the valet. Once their car pulled away with them in it, he sauntered over to the registration desk.

"Mr. Doring arrive yet?"

Chapter Twenty-one

The young woman blushed. "Yes. I'm sorry.
Things got crazy with people registering, and I forgot to
tell you. He's in his apartment."

"And that is…?"

"Oh, sorry! Go up the elevator to the fourth floor
and then take a right. It's the door at the end of the
hall." She picked up the phone. "Do you want me to
announce you?"

"No. I'd prefer he didn't come up with an excuse to
not see me."

Ryan headed to the elevator, punched in four, and
prayed the woman didn't decide her job depended on
her warning her boss.

He stepped out of the elevators and strode down
the hall to the right. Ten feet from the door, it opened
and out stepped a young curvy woman dressed in a
revealing dress.

"You promised we'd spend the week together," she pouted, looking back over her shoulder.

"Babe, I can't have you around here now that my wife has been murdered." Doring's voice barely carried down the hall to Ryan.

He moved quickly to the open door. "Excuse me." Ryan grasped the woman's arm, directing her back into the room. "I have several questions about that."

Doring glared at Ryan, and then the woman Ryan held by the arm.

"Who are you?" the woman asked, yanking her arm from his grasp.

"Detective Greer of the Weippe County Sheriff's Department. I'm in charge of investigating the murder of Paula Doring." Ryan pulled out his notepad. "And you are?"

"Tammy Smith. I don't know anything about Sidney's wife other than she died a few days ago." Ms. Smith backed away from Sidney. "I don't know what the police are doing investigating you but don't call me. I don't like the odds of being your girl."

She put a hand out as if to move Ryan out of the doorway. He made note of her comment about "the odds."

"Ms. Smith, where were you this past Friday afternoon?"

"I was in Seattle, preparing for my trip here." She tossed a seductive glance toward Doring. "Sidney and I had plans to spend this week together."

"You do know he is/was a married man?" Ryan couldn't believe the scruples of the people involved in this case.

"He was working on a divorce. That shrew he

married was spreading her legs for anything in pants and denying him." She took a step toward Doring, then seemed to have second thoughts.

Doring's face was a deep shade of red as he held his temper in check. The pulsing vein in his forehead and tightly fisted hands proved he didn't like Ms. Smith giving information so freely.

"Could I have your phone number in case I have any follow up questions?"

She recited her phone number. Ryan stepped aside, allowing her to leave. He shut the door of the apartment and leveled his gaze on Doring. "I have some questions for you, Mr. Doring."

Doring motioned for Ryan to enter the room farther and walked over to a small bar.

"Can I get you anything, detective?" The cool timbre of his words revealed Doring was barely holding in his anger.

"No, thank you." Ryan sat on a leather chair and waited for Doring to sit. Once the man was seated and sipping his drink, Ryan began.

"Did you have any interest in your wife's gallery besides giving it cash infusions every month?"

Doring leaned forward. "I don't know where you're getting your information, but I didn't give Paula any financial help with that damn gallery."

Ryan peered at the man. He peered back, unflinching. "You weren't putting money into the gallery account the beginning of every month?" Was the woman a call girl on the side?

"No. If she was putting money in you can bet it was probably made on her back. She sinks her claws in good and you don't realize what you've gotten yourself into until it's too late." The man drained his drink and stood. "You sure you don't want a drink?"

Ryan waved him off and pulled the sketch out of his pocket. When Doring sat back down, Ryan handed the sketch to him. "Do you know this man?"

Doring's eyes widened before they narrowed. "What does he have to do with my wife's death?"

"That's what I'm trying to figure out. Do you know him?"

"Yes. He's a private detective from Seattle I hired." Doring gulped his drink and set the glass on a side table. "I hired Terrance to come up with information on Paula that I could use in the divorce."

"Terrance? As in Terrance Baylor?" That was a hard name to forget. It was the same private detective Naomi had used to find her sister.

"Yes. If you know him, how come you didn't recognize him?" Doring started posturing like a CEO.

"I've only heard of him. Naomi Norton had him find her sister, Joyce."

Doring's eyes lit up, and he leaned forward. "You mean Terrance knew Joyce?"

"He apparently knew your wife as well. They had an argument the day before your wife was murdered and a witness says Paula said to him…" Ryan flipped through his notepad. "Your showing up is poor timing." He glanced up at Doring. The vein in his forehead was pulsing again. "Any idea what she meant by that?"

"Damn that Baylor. He's been telling me he's having trouble getting anything on Paula. Apparently he knew my wife." He stood up and kicked the side table sending the table and contents crashing across the room. "That whore was probably sleeping with him too!" He rubbed his hands over his face. "How could I have been so stupid?"

Doring stalked to the bar, turned over a glass, and poured more whiskey. He didn't bother with the ice and guzzled the liquid.

Ryan watched and waited. With luck, the liquor would give the man loose lips and thoughts. When he'd downed that glass, Ryan cleared his throat. Doring started at the sound and faced him.

"What can you tell me about your wife and Joyce Carter?"

Tears glistened in Doring's eyes. "Joyce was a sweet woman. Gorgeous inside and out. When she told me what her boyfriend had done, getting her hooked on drugs and making her do things she didn't want to do, my heart went out to her, and I tucked her under my wing. We were seeing each other, I thought secretly, waiting for some business to get finished so I could divorce Paula." He poured another drink, took a swallow, and the tears flowed freely down his cheeks. "Joyce was the woman who could make me monogamous. All I wanted was to be with her. I've never felt that way about another woman. Not even my wife."

Doring sat down and stared into his drink. "I made the mistake of suggesting she try for the job at the gallery. When I mentioned to Paula I'd take it as a favor if she'd help Joyce out, I more or less put the noose around Joyce's neck. I should never have put those two together. Paula was like a shark. If she smelled blood she went in for the kill. And Joyce was sweet and innocent for all that she'd been through."

"I heard that her boyfriend dumped her when Paula

started broadcasting Joyce's past around town."

The man sobbed. He dropped his drink on the floor and grasped his head. The amber liquid sloshed over his shiny black shoes. "I thought if I dumped Joyce, Paula would leave her alone. But that only made Joyce feel more vulnerable. Every time I tried to help her, I only pushed her toward her death." Doring peered up at him with red-rimmed eyes. "I'll go to my grave taking the blame for Joyce's death."

"Did you give her the overdose?"

"No! I know how getting her life back from drugs had given her an inner strength."

"Then you didn't kill her." Ryan decided to use the man's incapacitated state to get some more information. "Did you know your wife planned to marry Juan Lida after the divorce?"

Doring started laughing. His uproarious mirth took a minute to slow.

"You find that information funny?" Ryan had the same feeling when he'd heard the proclamation from Lida.

"Paula would never marry anyone who couldn't put more money into her bank account. She might have been sleeping with him and making him promises to do her bidding, but she would never have married him." He swung an arm out. "This is the lifestyle she likes. Her gallery could not give her this lifestyle and neither could that dime-store artist."

"She could have loved the man."

"Paula only loved two things: herself and money." Doring picked up the toppled cup from the floor and walked to the bar. "In the beginning, she was so hot and complying I'd thought I'd hit the jackpot. If I had to be hitched it wouldn't be so bad to have an experienced woman in my bed that said yes to all my wishes." A sardonic grin quirked his lips. "It was all a game to suck me in. A month after the marriage she showed her true side; selfish and conniving."

"Did you know what her profession was before you married her?" Ryan had to know if the man was so blinded by lust that he ignored the woman's past.

"She sold cosmetics at a large department store. I met her when I was getting perfume for my, at that time, girlfriend." Doring sat down. His gaze wasn't focusing. He looked ready to pass out.

"I would have thought a man like you would have done a background check."

"I did. I used Terrance Baylor." Doring's head snapped back. He pointed his chin at Ryan and peered down his nose. "What are you skirting around?"

"I have copies of your wife's arrest records. She was a drug addict and prostitute before she married you."

"Get out! Get out!" Doring flung his glass at Ryan. He not only missed, he tumbled to the floor.

Ryan closed the door and headed to the office to dig up all he could on Terrance Baylor. Specifically, his current vehicle and plate.

Chapter Twenty-two

*The man from the sketch had his face painted—one side red and one side black. Shandra watched from behind the warrior statue as the man opened crates and unwrapped works of art. He moved about searching. Ella's face appeared like a ghost in the darkness beyond the man and Shandra recognized the Doring Gallery. Why was he searching the packed art objects?*

*Ryan emerged from the darkness. A loud boom and flash of orange jolted her heart.*

Shandra shot to a sitting position and stared into the darkness of her bedroom. Her body shook as drying perspiration made her skin sticky and itch. She grabbed her cell phone and hit the on button. Light blinded her momentarily before she searched for Ryan's number. He'd told her to call if she had another dream. This time he was in it and in danger. With no regard to the time, she pushed the number and listened to the phone ring.

"Greer."

Ryan's scratchy voice made her wince.

"Sorry, to wake you, but you said to call if I had another dream."

Creaking sifted through the phone as he shifted. "Shandra?" A click sounded like a light switch. "What was it?"

"The man from the sketch—"

"Terrance Baylor."

"You know who he is? How is he connected to Sidney? Was he paid to kill Paula?" She had so many questions bouncing around in her head she felt motion sick.

"Whoa, I'll answer all that later. What happened in your dream?"

"The man, Baylor, had his face painted half red and half black as he searched the crated and wrapped art pieces in the back room at Doring Gallery."

Cursing hissed from the phone. "When we went back to the gallery and found Rowan, it didn't connect until now. The back room wasn't as neat and tidy as it was the first couple times we were there."

"Do you think he's already found what he was looking for?"

"I don't know. I think I know what he was looking for and there should still be traces." Clothing and movement rustled on the other end of the phone.

"What are you going to do?" He could be in danger if he went to the gallery. She woke before learning who shot the gun or if anyone was injured.

"Calling in a K-9 unit that is used to sniff out drugs."

"Drugs? You think Paula was dealing drugs?" That

possibility hadn't even entered Shandra's mind.

"It all points to that. She was a user, Rowan is still a user, and it would account for the monthly payment she received if she was the drop-off site." Grunts and labored breathing whistled in her ear.

"Shandra, I can't get dressed and keep talking. I'll call you when I learn something."

"Wait! Be careful. A gun shot woke me from the dream." She clutched the phone wishing she could keep him on while he did all his duties.

"Gunshot? On your property?" Anger and concern laced his words.

"No, in my dream. There was a gunshot. It shocked me awake. Be careful."

"I'll be careful, and I'll call."

"You promise?"

"I promise. Go back to sleep." His tone was gentle, intimate, like a lover slipping out of bed in the middle of the night.

The line went dead.

His gentle nudge for her to go back to sleep wouldn't do. There'd be no more sleep. Shandra glanced at the clock. Three a.m., she might as well get up. She clicked the light on the side table. Sheba lumbered to her feet, shoving her large head into Shandra's lap.

"Girl, it's going to take at least an hour for a K-9 unit to travel to Huckleberry, not to mention getting someone out of bed and ready to go." She stared at the big brown eyes peering back at her. "I think I'll take a shower and head to Huckleberry. I feel like a breakfast at Ruthie's." She kissed Sheba between the eyes and moved the bowling ball sized head out of her lap. "I might just swing by the gallery before breakfast."

~*~

Ryan shoved his right foot into his cowboy boot as he slipped his cell phone into the belt holster. He'd need evidence before he could call in a drug sniffing dog. The Sheriff wouldn't be happy if he heard the K-9 unit was called in because a woman had a dream.

He'd have to prove there was a need for the unit.

The motel he'd crashed at for the night was across the highway from the Jiffy Mart. Rather than throw suspicion on his vehicle parked by the gallery, he jogged across the highway and ducked into the alley that ran behind the Huckleberry Street businesses.

If there happened to be someone in the gallery, he wanted surprise on his side. The smell of old food accosted him as he walked behind Ruthie's. The back door stood open. Heat and a radio talk show drifted out the door. The woman must live upstairs to have closed the restaurant at nine and be back up this early to prep for the morning meal.

He crossed Second Street. The alley behind the jewelry store, a sandwich shop, and Dimensions Gallery was dark. Ryan slowed his gait and put his feet down lighter to muffle his boot heels hitting the pavement. At the corner of the building, he scanned First Street and the alley behind Doring Gallery. The street and alley were empty. No vehicles parked or moving on the streets. Baylor drove a silver sedan with a Washington plate.

Brisk steps took him across the street and to the back door of the gallery. He reached to insert the key into the lock. Crashing and scuffling deeper into the alley jerked his hand to his holstered Glock. He crept down the alley, quiet and slow. The noise grew louder. A thump and cat screams rang through the night.

Ryan stopped in the shadows beyond the light streaming from the open bakery door.

A man stepped out. "Go on! Get! You filthy alley cats!"

Something hit the dumpster. The screaming stopped, and two cats leaped out of the metal bin.

Ryan retraced his steps to the back of the gallery and inserted the key. The lock clicked and he entered. He walked to the opening between the back room and the gallery and shut the door.

The room had no windows, with the door shut the light wouldn't be seen from outside. He started in the far right corner and began a methodical search of every piece of shrink wrap, padding, and crates. If he could find a trace of any drug or by-products he could call in the K-9 unit and the drug task force.

~*~

Shandra never dallied while showering and this time was no exception. With her wet hair braided and dressed in old jeans, a light sweatshirt, and moccasins, she slid into her Jeep and headed down the mountain ten minutes after hanging up the phone.

Half-an-hour later, having driven faster than the speed limit, she cruised by the Huckleberry police station. Ryan's Tahoe wasn't there. She turned onto Second Street, drove by the gallery and peered into the alley. Ryan's SUV wasn't anywhere. Frowning, she made a circle of the block. As she turned right onto First Street, a silver car parked at the end of the alley behind the donut shop. The bakery had lights on.

"He could be getting early morning donuts." She

crept past the car, peering into the dark alley.
Something moved in the darkness. She parked ahead of
the vehicle and peeked in the windows of the bakery.
No customers, only the staff was in the shop.

Shandra eased her door closed and hurried to the
corner of the building. Early morning was a bad time to
try and rely on any of Mother Nature's light. The
business owners felt safe in this small town and only
had street lights on the two main streets, more for
ambiance than to guide anyone at night.

Using the light of the open bakery door, she made
her way past that establishment and was pitched into
darkness behind the boutique that was between Doring
Gallery and the donut shop. Her eyes started to adjust to
the darkness. Ahead the squeak of a hinge and light
filtering into the alley caught her attention. *How did he
get in? Did he have a key*? She pulled out her phone.
*Should I call Ryan*?

"How did he get the light on so fast?" she
whispered. The light had to be on when he opened the
door. Either he had an accomplice in the gallery already
or... *Ryan!*

Chapter Twenty-three

Ryan heard the click of the lock on the door and ducked behind the large crate he'd just opened. Whoever entered had a key. *I collected all the keys.* Did Lida withhold a copy? The way he doled them out to anyone who asked, he could have had an extra one or there was still unknown entities who had a key.

The intruder walked cautiously into the mess Ryan had made while searching. In his haste, he'd left a lot of debris strung about the room. To sneak up on the intruder would be foolish without a clear path.

The snick of a safety being released on a revolver rang loud and clear in the quiet room.

His heart pumped with adrenaline. He hadn't lived through the attack by gangs to end up dead in the back of an art gallery. Ryan shifted slowly to peer around the side of the crate.

Baylor.

He'd studied the sketch enough to know the man anywhere.

Baylor had his weapon ready as he scanned the room. The moment the man's head swiveled the other direction, Ryan lunged from his hiding spot and grabbed the arm holding the weapon.

The revolver went flying.

Baylor brought his free arm across, catching Ryan in the jaw. Pain shot through his teeth and into his skull.

Ryan wrenched the arm he had a hold on, down, and around behind the man's back, using a thumb hold to keep him from swinging again.

Baylor cried out and tried to grab Ryan with his free arm, but that only brought him more pain. Ryan slipped the cuffs on the wrist he held then snatched the other one. Once both hands were cuffed behind the man's back, Ryan spun him around.

His captive's eyes widened. The fierce fire and menacing frown were replaced by a grin curving his lips. "What the hell are you doing in here?"

Ryan stared at the man. "I'll be asking the questions. How did you get a key to this building?"

Baylor continued to grin and shake his head. "No. You have this wrong. I'm a good guy. Like you."

"I don't think—"

The door jerked open.

Ryan spun, his Glock in his hands ready to shoot.

Shandra's head peeked around the door jamb.

"What are you doing here?" Exasperation and terror rippled through Ryan's body at the thought he could have shot her.

Shandra's attention, on the hole in the end of the gun pointed at her, redirected to the face behind the

171

weapon. The tone and glower on Ryan's face pretty much told her this was probably not one of her smarter moves. But she wasn't about to let him know she had misgivings. Standing out in the alley she'd gone back and forth over what to do. When the scuffling noise died down, she decided if Ryan didn't have the upper hand her surprise entrance might give him a tactical advantage.

She stepped into the building, hands on hips, and stared back at Ryan.

"Did you find anything?"

Ryan nodded toward the man who looked like her sketch. "I found this."

The man had a rather disarming smile. "I don't know what you—"

"I'm taking you to the police station for questioning and trespassing." Ryan grabbed the man's arm and led him to the door. "Get the lights and shut the door," he said over his shoulder to her.

Shandra stared at Ryan's back. His gruff attitude was three-sixty from how he'd treated her up till now. Even when he hadn't completely ruled her out as a murderer. Had her impulse to come to the gallery been that much of a mistake? She turned off the lights, draping the room in black. The gray sky of dawn filtered through the still open door, guiding her. Stepping out the door, she slammed it shut and turned.

Ryan stood not two feet from her. "Come on," he ordered and set out leading his prisoner down the alley.

She'd planned to get her Jeep and head for breakfast at Ruthie's, but Ryan's tone irked as much as it commanded she comply.

The three of them moved at a brisk pace down the

alley and out to Second Street. No one said a word as Ryan held the door to the police station open for her. She entered and he pointed to the same chair she'd waited on the day before.

"Why am I here?" she asked.

"Because I want a word with you as soon as I deposit Mr. Baylor." Ryan nodded to the police officer at a desk. "Make sure she stays even if you have to cuff her to the chair."

Shandra glared at Ryan's back. He hadn't arrested her, so how could they keep her here? *I could walk out of here if I wanted.* She started to stand, but her gaze on Ryan and Baylor kept her seated. What would Ryan find out from the man? Was he at the gallery looking for drugs? Her curiosity overrode her anger. She sat in the chair watching the man be escorted into a small room. The other officer stood guard on the door when Ryan headed her direction.

Her guts churned and her mouth went dry at the determined and angry expression on Ryan's face. He didn't even stop as he grasped her arm, pulled her to her feet, and led her out onto the sidewalk.

"What were you thinking?" The words sounded as if his teeth were clenched together.

"I didn't want you to be alone while searching the gallery."

He dropped his hold on her arm and massaged the back of his neck with one hand. "That is poor logic. This is a police investigation. You need to stay the hell away."

"I was afraid the gunshot in my dream was meant for you. I had to be here to keep you safe. I'm the reason you were in the gallery."

He pulled his badge off his belt. "I'm paid to put my life on the line." He jammed the badge back on the belt and grabbed her arms. "I could have shot you when you opened that door."

His hands shook, and she felt his body vibrating only a foot away.

"I'm sorry. I was worried something would happen to you and wanted to be close to help." She ran a hand over his unshaven cheek. The haunted look in his eyes faded. "I didn't come here to make your work harder."

"Go home. I'll call you after I interrogate Baylor." He dropped his hands and took a step back.

"I have my heart and taste buds set on one of Ruthie's breakfasts." Her heart fluttered in her chest as their gazes met. "I'll be there when you get done with Baylor."

Ryan shook his head. "I don't know how long this will take."

Shandra smiled. "I'll be there whenever you show up." She drew in a deep breath, exhaled, and pivoted before she did something stupid like wrap her arms around him just to prove he was safe. She'd never been an overly demonstrative person. Putting her hand on his cheek had been uncharacteristic for her. Standing in front of the police station with this person wasn't the place to have her defenses breeched.

~*~

Ryan watched Shandra's backside until she turned the corner at the end of the block. That woman had a hold on him unlike any other. How he could want to throw her over his knee and paddle her one moment and want to kiss the living daylights out of her the next had him off balance.

He rubbed his face with his hands and entered the station. Without making eye contact with any of the other people, he walked to the table in the break room, picked up the file he'd composed on Baylor last night, and headed to the interrogation room.

He entered the room contemplating the strange behavior of Terrance Baylor. The man was slouched in a non-threatening position in one of the chairs. He smiled and eased up into a more respectful pose.

"Baylor, you seem to be a very busy person."

He spread his hands and leaned back in the chair. "I do tend to get around."

Usually a good judge of character, Ryan was getting mixed vibes from his suspect.

"Before you waste your time—," Baylor held out his hand as if to shake.

Ryan just stared at him.

Baylor shrugged. "Okay, who do you think I am?"

Ryan plopped the file open and started down the list. "You were in the military, when you were honorably discharged you started up a detective agency. It appears you travel around and have had several scrapes with the law. You are friendly with several people in drug cartels." Ryan slapped the file closed, "So what were you doing sneaking into a police secured area?"

Baylor smiled and raised his hands in an apologetic manner. "Looking for the same thing you were…drugs."

"At least you're honest. Did that get you off the hook the other times you were pulled in and questioned?" Ryan slapped his hand on the table, "It isn't going to work now!"

"Was that your girlfriend that interrupted our tussle? She's a looker."

Ryan sprang out of his chair and leaned on the table. His nose was only inches from Baylor's. "Don't draw her into this conversation."

"Relax. We're on the same side. Call the State Police and talk with the head of the drug task force. Ask him if he knows Terrance Baylor."

Ryan's gut said this man was a DEA agent. That's why he was getting mixed signals. But he wasn't going to believe the man until he had it confirmed. "Sit tight."

He left the room, pulled up the State Police number on his phone and asked for the captain in charge of the drug task team.

"Sir, do you know a Terrance Baylor?"

"I do, he's on a special assignment establishing the link between the high grade meth and new mix of heroin that is making its way into the rural areas. We've traced the source to Seattle."

Ryan rattled off Baylor's physical description.

"Yes, that's him. Why?"

"His description came up as a suspect in a murder investigation. When I caught him trespassing I brought him in for questioning."

"If he was sniffing around your murder, chances are your murderer is in the drug scene."

"Thank you for your time, Captain." Ryan pushed the off button and strode back into the interrogation room.

He took the seat across from the lounging DEA agent. "Why didn't you announce yourself to the local P.D.?"

"I'm not sure who in this town could be part of, or

being paid, by the cartel I'm after. They have their hooks into several small communities in Idaho and Washington. I can't always depend on the local police to not be on the take." Baylor leaned forward. "I didn't want to discuss it with your girlfriend around. You never know where the leaks are."

He understood the man's need for secrecy, but it irked he'd think Shandra was part of the drug problem.

"What do you know about Paula Doring?"

"I've had an eye on her off and on the last five years. She moved up fast from being a user to dealing. The gallery was a front for moving product. I was just getting into her good graces when she was killed."

"I have witnesses that say you two were intimate."

Baylor grinned like a teenager about to spill his conquests. "That woman felt the need to bed every male she dealt with. I think it came from her background as a hooker. Like it gave her control over them or something." He raised his hands. "But I never went that far and that made me one of her challenges."

"You had an argument with her behind the Quik Mart the day before she was killed. What was that about?" Even if this man was a DEA agent that didn't cross him off Ryan's suspect list. There was too much evidence that pointed to this man as being the murderer.

Baylor finally showed a tic of nervousness.

"She was surprised to see me in town since she knows me only as a private detective. One that was hired by her husband to dig up dirt on her before he married her."

Ryan raised an eyebrow. "Which I heard you gave her a clear background. Nothing at all like her police files show."

"That was to get her out of Seattle and see if she had really cleaned up her act. We were interested to see if she would work as an informant down the road." Baylor tapped an index finger on the table top. "I wasn't keen on the idea, especially when she got wind I'd given her soon-to-be husband such a glowing report. She became suspicious, and I had to do some things I'm not proud of all for the sake of bringing down a cartel."

Ryan knew the feeling. He'd done things he wasn't proud of as part of the gang task force in Chicago. "So what did Doring call you here for?"

"He wanted me to look into the death of a Joyce Carter."

Ryan had felt from the beginning these two cases were connected. "Why?"

"He didn't think she would have overdosed."

"Why did he wait until now to have you investigate?"

"He'd heard something that made him think she was murdered."

Ryan picked at the corner of the file on the table in front of him. "Did he give any specifics?"

"Only he thought his soon-to-be ex-wife was involved."

This was getting interesting. Not only did Paula slander the woman but it seems she wanted her out of her life as well. "This is all good information for my investigation. I have one more question for you. Were you in the gallery with Paula moments before she was discovered dead? Did you enact Sidney Doring's revenge?"

Baylor slammed his palms down on the table and glared at him. "I did not kill Paula Doring. I was in her gallery shortly before the body was discovered. She'd called me, saying she feared Sidney had discovered all her secrets and planned to use them against her in the divorce."

"Why did she call you?"

"To see if I'd told Sidney about her past and her connection to the Rafael cartel." Baylor slowly pulled his hands across the table toward him. "The Rafael cartel is the one that's been eluding me for years. I'd finally established the Doring Gallery as one of the drop-off sites, but I was still working out where the drugs went from here."

"So when you left the gallery Paula was still alive. Was she alone?"

Chapter Twenty-four

Shandra sat in Ruthie's diner picking at a cinnamon roll and drinking her third cup of coffee. She was so wired from the caffeine her eyeballs felt like they were jittery. What could be taking so long? If the guy did it, she had confidence Ryan could get it out of the man.

She peered out the window for the thousandth time gazing at the corner where Ryan would appear when he came to fill her in. A flashy SUV drove down Second Street. Her gaze latched onto the black/purple color. As an artist she admired interesting colors. Shandra smiled. That would be a great color to make some of her smaller vases.

The morning sunlight spilled into the front window of the vehicle, highlighting the inhabitants. The person in the passenger seat was Juan Lida. The driver was also Hispanic. What would Juan be doing riding around in such a nice car? There was a small Hispanic population in this part of the state but none of them could afford a flashy SUV.

Shandra dropped a ten on the table, grabbed her bag, and hurried out to the sidewalk. The SUV had continued down Second Street. She peered around the corner and saw them turn to the right on Pine Street. Shandra put her long legs to use, striding long and fast down Huckleberry Street to try and catch a glimpse of the SUV when it crossed First Street.

The vehicle turned up First Street. To avoid Juan noticing her, she stepped into the alcove of Dimensions Gallery and watched. The vehicle drove by slow. Both men's faces were turned toward Doring Gallery. What were they trying to see? The police tape still stretched across the front doorway. They made a left onto Huckleberry.

She stepped out of the alcove and watched as they turned to the left down Main Street. Were they circling the block? Peering down the alley? Shandra stayed on the corner until she saw the nose of the SUV turning back up First Street. She ducked back into her hiding spot and waited for them to drive by.

They didn't drive by. The SUV parked beside the business located behind the Doring Gallery. If she stepped out to the sidewalk, Juan might get suspicious. She had two choices. Wait for Ted and Naomi to open their store and let her in, or call Ryan and have him drive by and see what the two men were up to.

The time on her phone made the decision. Ted and Naomi wouldn't open the doors for two more hours. She found Ryan in her favorites list and dialed. Hopefully she wasn't interrupting his interrogation.

The phone went straight to voice mail.

"Hello Ryan? This is Shandra. Juan Lida and another man are sitting in a flashy SUV on First Street watching the Doring Gallery. I'm in the doorway of Dimensions Gallery. Call me back, please."

She hung up the phone feeling even less confident that she should be standing here keeping surveillance on the two in the SUV. Juan was Paula's assistant. Did he know there were drugs in the shipments? Was he waiting for a chance to cash in on what was still in there? She hadn't had a chance to ask Ryan if he'd found anything. Had Paula's involvement in drugs killed her?

Leaning into the corner where she could watch the two men through the glass door and a side window in the gallery, she wished she'd eaten breakfast instead of waiting for Ryan. All that coffee on a near empty stomach was burning her stomach lining.

~*~

Ryan's phone vibrated while talking with Baylor. He'd pushed the button sending the call to voicemail. Glancing at the recent calls, he noted it was Shandra. Did she get tired of waiting and head home? He hoped so. He punched the numbers and waited for her voice.

*Shit!* She wasn't supposed to play amateur detective.

"Baylor, do you know if a flashy black SUV has anything to do with your operation?"

"It's been seen hanging around when there is a shipment. Why?" Baylor buckled on his shoulder holster.

"It's sitting a block down from Doring Gallery." He wasn't about to involve Shandra. The DEA op already thought she could be a suspect.

"They're watching to see if there is any activity around the place." Baylor shoved his revolver into the holster.

"One of the men in the vehicle is Juan Lida." Ryan headed for the door. He had to get Shandra out of there and apprehend the two in the SUV.

Baylor matched him stride for stride as he ate up the sidewalk heading up Second Street.

"Why are you walking?" Baylor asked.

"Because it is less conspicuous. I have to get my informant out of there before I can move on the SUV."

"It's a civilian?" Baylor laughed. "You'd think a resort this size and famous would have a larger police force."

Ryan crossed the street. He stared at Dimensions doorway and could barely make out a form lurking in the shadows. He stayed close to the store fronts and slipped into the alcove.

Shandra turned to him her eyes wide. "I'm glad to see you. They've just been sitting in the SUV down there."

She nodded toward the inside of the gallery, and he noticed the good vantage point she had.

"How did you find them? You were supposed to be waiting for me at Ruthie's." He moved in closer to keep Baylor from seeing his informant. But the DEA agent had stayed across the street and was now crossing nonchalantly and walking in front of Doring Gallery.

"I was waiting for you and the vehicle caught my eye. Then I saw Juan in the passenger seat, and I became curious how a gallery assistant and not-so-talented artist would know someone in such a fancy car. So I kept an eye on them. They circled the block before stopping there."

"What did I tell you earlier about getting in the way of my investigation?" He put a hand on her upper arm.

"I know, but this just felt like they were up to something. And he is still a suspect isn't he?"

Her eyes peered into his, searching. For what he wasn't sure.

"Yes, he's still a suspect. In fact, even more than before. Baylor is a DEA agent. With his testimony I was able to get a drug sniffing dog here today. And I believe Paula's death had to do with her gallery being a drop-off for drugs."

Ryan looked up. "What the…?" Baylor was approaching the SUV.

"Do you trust him?" Shandra questioned softly.

"Not completely. There was a reason your grandmother put him in your dreams. But I don't know if it was because he is the killer and an adept liar or because he has a clue to the killer."

Shandra tugged on his sleeve, drawing his attention to her. "Why are you focusing on my dreams? They may not mean a thing."

Her furrowed brow and confusion in her eyes, drew him closer. He wiped a thumb across the furrows. "For them to be so vivid and you to see Baylor in them when you'd only drawn him…they mean something. Once you believe that you'll probably pick up on what your grandmother is telling you."

She shook her head. "Your belief in me is stronger than my belief in me."

He glanced at the SUV. Baylor leaned against the driver side door and chatted. Was he giving away that

Ryan was waiting them out? His gut soured.

"Shandra, go get in your Jeep and drive out of here."

"But he'll see me. My Jeep is still parked down by the bakery."

"Go back to Ruthie's and wait for me. Or have Treat give you a ride to your Jeep if he's in there." Ryan didn't like the way Baylor had stopped leaning. He glanced toward the doorway where he and Shandra hid.

"Go now!" Ryan grasped her arm and pushed her away from the doorway and toward the restaurant.

She started to comment but stopped when she glanced over his shoulder.

"Go!"

She jogged down the street, and he returned his attention to the SUV. Baylor was backing up as the driver of the vehicle stepped out. He had a hand in his jacket pocket and the pocket was held away from his body. *The driver had a gun on Baylor.*

Ryan pulled out his phone and pressed the button for the local P.D.. "I need back up on First Street near the Doring Gallery." He replaced the phone and backtracked down the street and around the block to arrive on First Street behind the SUV. If Juan looked in the side-view mirror he could warn the other man, but it appeared his attention remained on the two men on the sidewalk.

From his vantage point walking up behind the vehicle, Baylor was arguing with the driver.

When Ryan spotted the police vehicle round the corner, he took up a stance and called out, "Police, put your hands in the air."

The driver tried to get back in the SUV, but Baylor

shoved the door closed and grabbed the man's arm, wrenching it behind his back. Ryan cautiously approached the passenger side.

"Lida, put both hands out the window," Ryan called.

"I am only visiting with a friend," Lida said from inside the vehicle.

"Then put your hands out and I'll believe you aren't up to anything." Ryan could see the man's face in the rearview mirror. His gaze caught Ryan's, and he put his hands out the window. Ryan caught movement in the back seat. *There were more than two!*

He ducked as a shot shattered the glass. The tinted windows hadn't allowed him to see more than the two in the front.

"Get out now or I'll put a round into the back!" Baylor shouted as Ryan moved to the rear fender, ready to shoot or take down whoever came out of the back. Officer Blane was crouched behind his car door with a shotgun pointed at the front of the SUV.

The backseat doors opened at the same time and two men stepped out of the back. The man on Ryan's side had an automatic rifle. Before the man leveled the barrel, Ryan let loose with a round kick, knocking the weapon from the man's hands. The suspect started toward him but stalled at the sight of Ryan's Glock pointed at the man's head.

"Turn around and put your hands behind your head." Ryan heard a similar scuffle on the opposite side of the vehicle. Once the man was handcuffed, Ryan slammed the back door and yanked open the front.

Lida made an attempt to hide a .45 between the seat and console. Ryan grabbed the weapon and pulled

Lida out of the SUV. He waved Blane over. "Lend me your cuffs."

All four men were cuffed and stuffed into the back seat of the police car. Ryan rode shot gun with Blane. Baylor said he'd lock up the SUV and wait for his people to search for evidence.

As soon as the four were in a holding cell, Ryan punched in a number.

"Hello?" The relief in Shandra's voice in that one word gave him hope they might become more than friends.

"There were four men in the SUV. I have them in custody. You might as well go home, I'll be busy here for the rest of the day." He had been looking forward to spending time with Shandra but his job came first— always.

"Will you be done by dinner time?" The invitation in her voice put a smile on his face.

"What time would that be?"

"Seven. My place."

"I'll be there." He hung up looking forward to a nice dinner and good company.

~*~

Good thing I'm still in town. Shandra dropped another ten on the table at Ruthie's to pay for the breakfast she could finally swallow after Ryan called and headed out the door. There were a couple items she wanted to pick up at the store for dinner tonight. First she had to get her Jeep. Walking down Huckleberry Street, she noticed a lot of commotion as she passed First Street. There was a dark van pulled up behind the SUV, a dark car in front of the SUV, and half a dozen people all around and inside the vehicle.

The man, Baylor, was giving directions. She hadn't decided if she liked the guy or not, so she kept on walking. At the bakery, she stepped in and purchased shortcakes. Everyone liked strawberry shortcake.

She unlocked the passenger side of her vehicle and placed her purchase on the passenger seat. When she turned from closing the door, she spotted Naomi watching the people investigate the SUV. She must have seen all the commotion and came out to take a look. Shandra started to raise her hand to catch her friend's attention when Naomi pivoted and hurried back to her gallery.

Shandra climbed into her Jeep and headed to the grocery store. She planned to impress Ryan with her cooking and ply him with beer or wine, whichever he drank when off duty, and try to find out more about the case.

Chapter Twenty-five

Ryan's phone rang as he started the bumpy ride up Shandra's drive.

"Hello?"

"Where are you at? We haven't heard from you in a while." Bridget's bubbly voice made him smile.

"You know I'm working a case at Huckleberry." His senses went into double-time. "What has Cathleen said to you?"

"Nothing. Just it was reported that you had an interesting chat with a woman outside the police station today." The singsong in her voice reminded him of the old kissing chant his sisters sang when they found out he liked a girl.

"Who told her—" It had to be the dispatch at Huckleberry. They probably know one another. He couldn't have his own life as long as he was in Idaho. That was why he'd gone to Chicago.

"Well, who is she? Is it the same person you told Conner you'd bring as a date to the wedding?"

"Listen, I just pulled up at her house. We're having dinner. How about I call you tomorrow and give you the info on how it all went." He hung up and smiled. He'd never tell his little sister all about his dates. By the time she figured out he wasn't calling he'd have had a nice evening.

He parked in front of the house and slipped out of his shoulder holster, locking it in his glove box. Sheba came bounding around the side of the house. Now that he knew the dog wasn't a threat, he stopped and enjoyed her comical crouching approach.

"Hey, girl. Where did you learn your moves?" He scratched her wide head and looked up when he heard footsteps approaching.

"Come on around back. It's such a nice summer day, I'm barbequing." Shandra pivoted.

He followed her attractive denim backside to the back yard.

A patio created with what appeared to be local rock made a picturesque setting behind the log home. A hammock hung between two pine trees, a porch swing sat to the side of the picnic table, and a smoking charcoal grill sat at the end of the table. A cooler sat on the ground at the other end of the table.

"This could be a photo in a magazine." He admired the way it all blended with the mountain behind.

"I have to admit, I added this area to the house. There was a lawn with lots of flower beds. I don't have a green thumb and don't have a lot of time for outside chores, so to make this area useful and appealing I added the patio." She smiled and opened the cooler.

"Beer or wine?"

"Beer, please."

She held up a dark and light ale.

He pointed to the dark. She handed it to him, pulling out a fruity wine cooler for herself.

Ryan took a seat on the porch swing. It was the first relaxing moment he'd had since arriving in Huckleberry. He had to admit, he enjoyed watching Shandra turn the meat on the grill and move in and out of the house bringing side dishes.

"You don't have to wait on me. I could have walked into the kitchen and filled my plate." He wanted her to sit and visit, but he could sense she was intent on making the meal special.

Finally, she said, "The meal's ready. Come have a seat."

He sat down to perfectly cooked T-bone steaks, baked potatoes, steamed vegetables, and a broccoli salad. "This looks wonderful. The last time I had a home barbeque was over a year ago at my sister's house."

Shandra sat down across from him and smiled. The twinkle in her eyes made his heart speed up.

"You're welcome. I couldn't let a beautiful day like today fade away without enjoying it all the way to the end." She offered the steak plate to him.

"This is what I needed after today." He planned to share the information with her about the men in the SUV, but he also wanted to see how interested she was in the men.

She dished up the sides onto her plate and thoughtfully started cutting the steak. Finally, she lifted her gaze to his. "Thank you for calling me as soon as the situation was under control." Her eyelashes fluttered down then back up. "I heard a gunshot while sitting in Ruthie's." She reached over and touched his hand. "I was thankful when you called."

The touch and her concern elevated his attraction to her. As if it wasn't already to its peak.

"You're welcome. I had a feeling you hadn't left town." He turned his hand and captured hers.

"I couldn't without knowing the men were caught and you were fine." She slid her hand out of his and took a bite of her steamed vegetables.

"They are part of a drug cartel Baylor is after."

Her eyes widened, and she stared at him. "Juan is part of a drug cartel?" She frowned. "He seemed so…"

"Whipped?"

"Yeah, like he couldn't make a decision without someone telling him what to do." She placed a bite of meat in her mouth and chewed thoughtfully. "Why did he give Naomi a key if he was helping Paula hide drugs in the gallery?"

That's what he liked about Shandra. Her mind was always thinking. "When Naomi threatened him with INS he had to go along or someone might get suspicious."

"Did he kill Paula?" Shandra shuddered.

"No, I don't think Juan did. As you said he doesn't appear to think for himself. The other three appeared to be surprised to learn Paula was killed. Those three could have easily done the deed. She apparently had been working her way up the cartel to where even the drug lord was giving her high praises."

Shandra put down her eating utensils and picked up her wine and took a sip. "Then we're back to the beginning. Who would want Paula dead?"

"Why don't we call it quits on trying to solve the murder for tonight?" He tipped up his beer and took a good swallow. When he put the bottle down, she was smiling.

"I think that's a good idea. So tell me more about these siblings you have."

Ryan spent the remainder of the meal talking about growing up in a family of four children in a rural area which made them constant companions during their youth.

Shandra saw that even though Ryan called his siblings butt-in-skis and trouble makers, he had a special bond with each of them. Even the brother marrying his ex-girlfriend. There had been many times over the years she'd wished for siblings. But her mother and stepfather had found it trying enough to raise her.

She stood and gathered up the dishes.

"Let me help." Ryan stood and stacked dishes.

"Thank you." She carried her share into the kitchen and he followed.

"What were you thinking about out there? You looked a million miles away." He stood beside her as they both placed the dirty dishes in the sink.

"Life. Just life." She gave him her best forced smile and he frowned.

"What about your life don't you like?" He leaned a hip against the counter only inches from her.

"The loneliness. It seems like I've been alone my whole life." *Whoa, that popped out unexpected.*

"Is that why you're like a fierce mama bear when you defend Naomi?"

"I guess. Could be. I never thought about it

before." She glanced up to see if he felt pity for her. Instead she saw a sadness that wasn't a thing like pity. "I never voiced my loneliness out loud before."

He cupped her chin. Slivers of heat prickled her skin where he touched.

"Are you sure you don't crave the solitude? You did pick an isolated area and ranch to live."

"I do crave solitude, but there are days when I wish I had someone to give me a hug or tell me my latest creation was beautiful or needed something." She stared into his eyes. "Those are different than solitude."

He drew her into an embrace, leaning her against his broad chest. "Any time you want a hug all you have to do is ask."

They stood together, arms around one another, his head resting on hers. Shandra let her body melt against his strength and savor the warmth and woodsy scent of him.

The clatter of dishes on the patio broke them apart. Ryan exited before her. Raccoons scattered to the trees as Sheba raised her head from her spot in the shade of the house.

"It appears the raccoons enjoyed your dinner as much as we did." Ryan stacked the remaining, now empty dishes. He nodded toward Sheba. "She's not much of a watch dog."

Shandra laughed. "Sheba picks her battles and the raccoons have outfoxed her enough she just ignores them."

When the dishes were finished Shandra led Ryan out to the porch swing. They sat side by side their shoulders and thighs touching as he talked about life in Chicago, and she told stories of her escapades growing up on the ranch in Montana. The vermilion sky slowly faded to dark blue and twinkling stars popped out.

Ryan put an arm around her shoulders. Shandra leaned her head on his shoulder. It had been a long time since she'd had this peaceful of an evening. Even longer since she'd shared it with anyone other than Sheba.

"Thank you," she whispered.

"For what?" His hand massaged her shoulder.

"For believing me that first day. For not thinking I'm crazy to explore my dreams." She shifted to peer into his eyes. "I'm still not convinced they mean anything, but I have to follow Ella's directions to see if they are. In my heart, I feel the connection to her and her people, but in my head…I'm still battling the prejudice of my mother and stepfather."

His eyes flared when she talked of her doubts.

"I'm happy that your heart is telling you to believe. I've found that most times your gut and your heart know more than your head." He lowered his lips to hers.

The kiss was soft, gentle, and set her heart pounding like the ceremonial drums.

Ryan drew away from her and slowly lifted his arm. "I had a wonderful time. You're a great cook, and I enjoyed the company more than I have anyone in a long time." He stood and drew her to her feet. "Promise if you have any dreams or notice anything strange you'll call me."

"You are the only person I can call. Anyone else would think I'm crazy if I told them about my dreams."

He cupped her chin and kissed her one more time, slow and thorough. "I'll call you tomorrow."

Shandra nodded slightly as she savored the way his touch and kisses made her body content. "I'll be here working."

He faded into the darkness as he rounded the house. Sheba rose to her feet and followed.

Shandra sat back down in the swing and smiled. She might have finally found a man who embraced her heritage rather than treated it like a disease.

Chapter Twenty-six

*Shandra walked along a stream, her thoughts filled with the things in her life that make her happy: Sheba, her art, the mountain, Ryan, and horses. As she thinks of each one, they appear before her. She touches each, noting the things about them that she loves. She slides her hands up Ryan's bare chest and sighs. The horses paw and snort as if to tell her not to go on. But the need to see more drives her forward.*

*Paula stands at the edge of a cliff, dangling Joyce into the emptiness by her hair. Shandra's heart pounds with fear. She tries to hurry forward, but Paula releases Joyce and she drops. Paula cackles and two men appear. One has the spear from the statue sticking out of his back pocket. The two men talk and point at Paula who stares down into the canyon where she dropped Joyce.*

*Shandra hides behind a tree, trying to get a good*

*look at the two men, but their faces remain a blur. One leaves and the other, with the spear in his pocket, approaches Paula. They embrace, disrobe, and have sex. Shandra turns her head from the scene. Not comfortable with intimacy, she wants to flee, but Ella is sitting on her shoulder, whispering, "Don't leave, your answer will come."*

*The intimate sounds die away, and she turns back around. Paula is alone and motionless. Twigs are scattered around her body and the spear is protruding from her chest.*

Shandra's heart raced, and she gasped for air as if she'd climbed the mountain. "What are you telling me this time, Ella?" Before the details faded, she grabbed up a journal and pen and started writing down the dream.

"If only I had seen the faces on the men."

Sheba climbed up on the bed and lay down beside her. Her caring, brown stare was what Shandra needed right now. A hug from a certain detective would have been nice too. Her mind wandered to the kisses they shared and how nice his arms had felt when he held her.

"Should I call Ryan now?" She glanced at the clock. *Two.* No, this wasn't anything that couldn't keep. After all, she didn't have a clue who the men were. This could wait until daylight hours. She'd work in the morning and go to town for lunch and see if Ryan could join her, and then she'd tell him about the latest dream. It had to be a clue.

~*~

Shandra finished glazing the last batch of vases. She and Lil placed them in the kiln.

"You're a lot brighter today than I've seen you in a

198

while," Lil said, closing the kiln lid. "Wouldn't happen to be your dinner guest putting that glow in your cheeks?"

"Could be. Or it could be I'm learning to accept who I am." Shandra set the heat on the kiln.

"It appears to me that your gentleman friend is good for you spiritually and physically." Lil scooped up Lewis and headed to the door.

"What do you mean?" Shandra had woke this morning feeling more light-hearted and carefree than she had since adulthood gave her the chance to strike out on her own.

"I've just seen good changes in you since meeting this man." Lil slipped out the door with Lewis around her neck like an orange fur collar.

"Am I this happy and content because of Ryan?" she asked Sheba and stared at the dog. "Maybe. If his friendship can keep me walking on clouds and loving life, then I need to make an effort to stay in contact after he finds the murderer."

She stepped out of the studio with Sheba on her heels. Her cell phone was in her hand before she consciously decided to give Ryan a call.

~*~

Ryan scrolled through the information Cathleen sent him on Sidney Doring's financials and the divorce papers. It appeared Paula felt entitled to nearly everything Sidney owned. The only thing she was leaving him with was his shares of the lodge. "That would make a man want to find a solution."

"What would?"

He looked over his shoulder and wasn't pleased to find Baylor studying the monitor. Ryan hit a button and made the information go away. "Paula was after everything in the divorce."

"Sounds about right." Baylor pulled up a chair. "Thought you might like to know we found the two art pieces that had drugs stashed in them. The shipping addresses were still intact and I have a team headed to each of the places to see what they can find out."

"But that doesn't tell you where they were being shipped to and if that is what got Paula killed."

"True, but Juan is willing to roll on the cartel if we give him a new identity and a safe place to live." Baylor slapped him on the back. "I have a way of swaying people to see they would be better off by narcing."

A bell clanged in Ryan's head. "Did you have anything to do with Dale Young getting a light sentence?"

Baylor's good humor lessened. "Dale who?"

Ryan's adrenaline rushed. The agent was stalling. "The drug pusher who was Joyce Carter's boyfriend. When I read the report I couldn't believe he was given such a light sentence."

The agent's face wasn't as stony as his steadfast gaze.

"He might have made a deal. I was working a different angle." The man's face gradually lightened until he no longer sported a tan.

"What angle were you working? The one that helped Paula nab a rich man for a husband?" He had the agent off balance. That was a good time to launch an assault. "Did Paula and Joyce know one another back then?"

"No, Paula had pulled herself out of the gutter before Joyce came along."

"Then why would Joyce say she couldn't run from her past?" He narrowed his eyes at the agent. "She couldn't have just meant Paula's vicious comments or the photos that showed Joyce was high when they were taken."

Baylor blanched again. Did he have something to do with the photos?

"Have you seen the photos Paula was using to shame Joyce?"

He ducked his head. "We raided Young's place on a night he was 'filming'." He shook his head. "Those photos were the evidence Joyce needed to get out of the guy's clutches. I saved a couple to give her, but they came up missing before I discovered where she'd hidden."

Ryan glared at the man. "I find it suspicious that they ended up in the hands of the woman you were supposedly using as an informant. What did she have on you that would make you hand over the photos?" He stared at the man in front of him. "Better yet, don't tell me and get the hell out of my sight. I've never been a fan of law enforcement people who make their own rules."

Baylor stood, but he had a lethal expression leveled on Ryan. "One of these days you're going to choose your righteousness over staying alive or keeping someone you love alive. See what you do then."

The man stormed out before Ryan could tell him he'd already walked the fence between good and evil and came out scarred but could sleep nights.

His phone rang. "Greer."

"It's Shandra. Any chance I can persuade you to join me for lunch at Ruthie's?"

He smiled just hearing her low sultry voice. This woman was special, and he planned to take things good and slow to not scare her off. Besides her having problems acknowledging her heritage, she had other demons she was working on.

"I could be persuaded if you could meet me at the lodge. I have some more questions for Mr. Doring."

"I had a dream last night. But some of the people in it were unclear. One had the spearhead in his back pocket." Shandra's tone expressed she was starting to believe in her dreams. Or at least the symbolism.

"Meet me at the lodge at twelve thirty."

"I'll be there."

Ryan punched the off button and opened the screen back up on the computer. He would need all the dirt he could dig up on Doring when he went back to question the man.

~*~

Shandra changed out of her work clothes and into something a little more flattering. It was a couple hours until she was to meet Ryan, but she had some other errands to run before lunch. Sheba stood beside the Jeep as she exited the house. The sad eyes and tilt to the animal's head zinged straight to Shandra's heart.

"You can go. Just don't slobber on my head." She opened the back door, and Sheba bounded into the back seat, talking excitedly.

Shandra laughed, rolled down the window, and closed the door. She slid in behind the steering wheel and patted the big head that popped between the front seats. "Keep the drool out the window."

In town, Shandra ran her two quick errands and drove to Dimensions. She'd received an email from a person she didn't know who said they'd dealt with Ted and Naomi before. She wanted to make sure it was a legitimate gallery asking to put her work on consignment.

She parked in the alley next to Naomi's car. Hooking the leash on Sheba, she peered across the street to the alley behind Doring Gallery. There were vans loading up boxes and crates. "Are they taking all the art pieces?" She had one vase in there. She'd rather have it in another shop than sitting in some evidence locker.

"Come." Shandra led Sheba across the road and into the alley. A woman in a dark pant suit spotted her. She walked toward them with a stern set to her mouth. When Shandra didn't stop, the woman put a hand up, palm facing Shandra.

"Stop. This is a federal investigation."

"I'm just going to the donut shop," Shandra said innocently.

"You'll have to go around. This alley is off limits to civilians."

Shandra craned her neck. "Are you loading up all the artwork?"

"No, just the items in the back room. Now move along."

Shandra pivoted and clicked her tongue to Sheba, who was still staring at the woman. Good news. They weren't taking all the artwork. Hopefully she'd get a call soon saying she could come pick up her vase. "But who is going to call?" Paula was dead. Juan was in jail, and Sidney didn't have anything to do with the gallery. Or would he now that his wife was dead. "Wouldn't he be the beneficiary?"

"What are you talking about?"

Shandra looked up. Ted stood at the sidewalk.

Sheba tugged on the leash to get a pat on the head from Ted.

"I was wondering out loud about who would call and ask me to pick up my vase. Would Sidney, now that he's the beneficiary after Paula's death?"

Ted shrugged. "I don't know, but those people have been hauling stuff out of there since yesterday. I can't believe there was that much stuff in there." He led the way to the back door of his gallery.

Shandra entered and tied Sheba to the leg of the work table. It was cooler in here than waiting for her in the Jeep. At the lodge, she could instruct the valet to park the Jeep in the shade with the windows part way down.

She followed Ted into the gallery. Naomi was working on the computer.

"We have—" Ted said.

"Oh! You startled me!" Naomi clicked off the keyboard before turning her attention to them.

"I stopped by to ask if either of you have heard of this gallery in Jackson Hole." Shandra handed the slip with the name of the gallery and the owner to Naomi.

She handed it to Ted. "I think you talked to her about a year ago. She called asking about an artist who had given our name as a reference."

Ted shook his head. "This isn't ringing any bells. Pull the gallery up on the computer." He reached around Naomi and hit a button.

"No!" Naomi swat his hands away.

But not before the last information flashed on the screen.

"Why are you looking into court records for Washington State?" Ted asked.

"Hearing the rumors about Paula being connected to drugs made me think maybe she had a connection with Dale Young, Joyce's boyfriend." Naomi's shoulders slumped. "I knew his sentence was light for what he'd been convicted of. When I asked on some free legal sites they say he probably turned evidence and that's why he had a light sentence."

Ted put his hands on Naomi's shoulders and massaged. "But he was still in jail when Joyce was killed. He couldn't have done it."

"No, but he could have had someone else do it for him. Someone he knew before Joyce." Naomi glared at her husband. "I know you keep telling me to let this be, but I can't. Joyce would not have overdosed. She was proud of getting clean and working toward a better life." She grabbed Shandra's hands. "I want whoever took my sister's life to pay. Even if I spend my whole life trying to discover the truth."

"Naomi, this isn't good for your health. Joyce wouldn't want you to get sick." Ted reached out to shut the computer off.

"No! I'm finally getting into the records that have Paula's maiden name on them."

Shandra motioned to the computer monitor, "Naomi, why don't you go make me a cup of tea and let me take a look at these for you. Sometimes fresh eyes see things that might have been missed." She gently maneuvered Naomi away from the desk and took the warm seat.

As Ted navigated his wife to the back room, Shandra began scanning the information Naomi had accessed. The woman must have majored in computer science because she had gotten into information the public wouldn't normally have access to.

There were not only documents stating Paula was helping the DEA, she found a reference to plastic surgery and vocation of artist under Young's information. He'd turned evidence against the cartel and had been given a new life complete with a face lift.

Knowing the degradation he'd put Joyce through and the fact he sold drugs, Shandra had a feeling he wasn't using his new life to become a model citizen. He could be anyone who moved into the community in the last six months.

"Have you found anything of interest?" Naomi set a cup of tea on the corner of the desk for Shandra and kept one for herself.

"Yes." Shandra filled Naomi in on all she read about Dale Young.

"That's the worst case of justice being screwed I've ever heard!" Naomi clanked her cup and saucer together as she placed them on the desk.

"It does make you wonder about the system." Shandra clicked the screen away and looked at the clock. "I have to scoot. I have a lunch date at the lodge."

"Please tell me it isn't with Sidney Doring."

"No, it isn't. It's with Detective Greer."

"Does he still suspect me?" Naomi's voice shook with worry.

"I don't believe he does." Shandra couldn't help the singsong tone in her voice.

Naomi's face brightened. "You like him! He must be liking you back for you to be this excited." Naomi hugged her. "I'm so happy for you. You haven't had a man in your life since you moved here."

"You don't mind he once thought of you as a suspect?"

"Not if he makes you this happy." Naomi waved her hands. "Go enjoy your lunch."

"Thanks! I plan on it."

Shandra said good-bye to Ted and untied Sheba. Out in the Jeep, she took one more look at the activity behind the gallery and wondered if they weren't also checking each piece on display. It wouldn't take two days to clear the back room out with all the people they had milling around.

Shifting into gear, she sailed out of the alley and down the street toward Huckleberry Highway and the lodge. The clock on her dash read twelve-twenty. She'd roll in right on time.

Chapter Twenty-seven

Shandra gave the valet instructions for Sheba and entered the lobby of the Huckleberry Lodge. She wasn't clear if she was to wait in the lobby for Ryan or get them a table in the restaurant. Indecision kept her rooted to the side of the entrance. It proved to be a good spot to watch all the comings and goings of the lodge. The vantage point showed a clear view of who got on and off the elevators. Who went down which hall and who came in the front door.

She sat on an overstuffed ottoman and took in the show. Staff moved about doing chores and errands. Guests went up and down the elevators and in and out the entrance. Oscar Rowan entered the lodge. She leaned back, to make herself blend into the fichus behind her. Something about his clothing was familiar. What was it? He entered an elevator, and she watched the numbers. All the way to the top floor.

Was he staying in the lodge? It seemed a bit expensive for an artist who had yet to make a big sale.

The familiar sound of cowboy boots caught her attention and she smiled. Ryan paused in the lobby, scanning the area. She stood and walked over to him.

"Are you looking for someone?" she asked just as she came up behind his shoulder.

His alert, stiff posture relaxed before he pivoted and smiled. "Yes. You."

The welcome in his eyes made her heart thump loudly in her ears.

He motioned toward the restaurant, and she walked beside him. His hand settled warm and secure on her lower back as he followed her. At the restaurant entrance, she looked over her shoulder to smile at Ryan.

She caught a glimpse of a man walking away. An envelope stuck out of his back pocket and the image of her dream popped into her head. He was the man with the spearhead in his pocket. It was the same type of pants, same body shape, even the back of the head was a match.

She clutched Ryan's shirt sleeve.

"What is it?" Ryan peered down into Shandra's face, drained of color. She stared over his shoulder. He wrapped an arm around her waist and spun them both around. A man was exiting the lodge.

"That man was in my dream."

He barely heard her whispered statement.

The waitress walked up. "Two?"

"Yes. In a private corner, please." Ryan ignored the knowing smile on the older woman's face and led Shandra to a table in the far corner of the establishment. "This will do, thank you."

The corner, padded booth was cozy. He nudged Shandra in, and sat down, scooting her over until they sat side by side, watching the activity of the restaurant. The waitress took their drink orders and left.

"Tell me about your dream." Ryan grasped Shandra's hand and laced his fingers with hers under the table as she told him about two men in her dream.

"That man who just walked out of here was one of them. He had on the same type of pants and the envelope sticking out of his pocket reminded me of the spearhead that was in his back pocket." She added, "In my dream, there were twigs scattered around when the two met."

"Twigs and Oscar Rowan. Remember when we caught him in the office and there were pieces of white sticks all over the floor?" Ryan asked.

"Yes. Do you think the twigs are referring to those sticks?"

"Could be. The sculpture those sticks made was of a man and woman having sex. Do you remember the saying on the base?"

"Yes. 'My love twines around you like a clinging vine, giving you nourishment.' It's sweet and corny at the same time." She wrinkled her nose.

He wanted to lean over and kiss the tip of her nose but refrained from any such display in public. He was still working a case and it did involve the woman sitting beside him.

"If Rowan found out about any of Paula's other lovers, he might have become enraged and killed her in a fit of jealousy. From my interviews with him, he came across as a man with a lot of rage." At the time Ryan had thought it was genuine but now he wondered if it wasn't an act.

"When you questioned him, did he give you a reason to consider he was the murderer?"

The waitress returned with their drinks. "Have you decided what to order?"

Shandra shook her head and dutifully picked up the menu. He did the same. They both ended up selecting the day's special of tomato soup and a grilled turkey sandwich. The waitress left, and they both watched her walk across the restaurant.

"I had a feeling he wasn't being truthful, but I couldn't catch him up in anything." If the man was the murderer he was an accomplished liar, and that would make it harder to get the truth from him. "I wonder where he was coming from."

"He went up to the top floor when he came in." Shandra extracted her hand from his as the waitress returned with their soup.

"Doring lives on the top floor." Ryan put his napkin on the table and slid out of the booth. "I'll be right back."

Shandra nodded, but her eyes reflected she didn't believe he'd be back in a minute.

Ryan hurried out to the front desk. The older clerk was on duty.

"Are there any rooms on the top floor for guests to reserve?" He forced his face to remain friendly and not show the adrenaline that pumped through him. This may finally be the break they needed to find the murderer.

"Only the two honeymoon suites and Mr. Doring's rooms are on the top floor." She replied and aimed her attention to the ringing phone.

"Thank you." He hurried back to Shandra. "Unless Rowan recently married or was visiting a newlywed couple the only other person on the top floor is Sidney Doring."

Shandra twirled her spoon around in the soup. "That envelope wasn't in his pocket when he went up. I bet he was paid for something." She took a bite of soup and pointed her spoon at him. "I bet it was murder."

~*~

Thirty minutes later, Ryan rode the elevator to the top floor with Shandra. He'd prefer to question Sidney alone, but she had a point. She was the witness to Rowan traveling to the top floor.

The elevator lunged to a stop. "Remember, you are to get the hell out of here if he gets violent." The doors swished open.

"Yes. But he won't."

"How can you be so confident?"

"Because other than the little incident at the art event, Sidney knows how to control his emotions." Shandra's smile was a bit wobbly.

He didn't have time to tell her about the way the man broke down the last time he was questioned.

Ryan knocked on the door to Doring's suite.

"Just a minute. I had to wait for—" Doring answered the door. "Oh, I thought you were room service. I called down my order thirty minutes ago." He held his hand on the door and stood in the opening, barring entrance. "What do you want?"

"I have some questions for you." Ryan took a step to enter, but the man stood steadfast.

"I don't want her in here. She'll probably come up with some lie and get me arrested again." Doring glared at Shandra.

Ryan stepped between the two. "This is official police business having to do with the death of your wife."

"Then why is that bitch here?" Doring pointed his chin at Shandra.

This was the reason why Ryan hadn't wanted Shandra to come along. "If she leaves will you allow me to question you?"

"Wait a minute, you can't—" Shandra put her hand on his arm and tried to push him out from in front of her.

He spun. "I can and I will," Ryan said the words firm and with force. Then as she started to sputter, he mouthed the words, "Just go. Please."

"I have information you need while questioning him." Shandra spun on her heel and marched to the elevator.

*Damn!* Ryan's gut soured at her words. Her parting remark was sure to get her in Doring's crosshairs if he was the one who murdered Paula.

He erased any expression and faced Doring. "Can we talk now?"

The man moved out of the doorway and headed straight for the bar. He raised a glass. "You want anything?"

"No." Ryan pulled out his notepad. "Could you tell me what kind of business you and Oscar Rowan have together?"

Doring's hands stopped pouring liquor into a glass for only a split second before he looked up and smiled. "I purchased one of his bronze statues."

"Is that why he left here with an envelope of

money today?"

Doring raised the glass to his lips, took a swallow, and smiled. "Yes. It was a payment for the statue he is having delivered next week."

"I'd like to see the paperwork." This line of questioning was getting him nowhere. He'd have to check the man's financials and see where the money came from and then talk with Rowan and see if a statue really was purchased.

"Are you now part of the law group that polices art transactions? I've never had to prove my art purchases to anyone but my accountant." Doring's face hosted a smarmy smile.

Realizing this was a waste of time, Ryan turned to the door. He stopped and spun around. "Now that your wife is dead who is in charge of the gallery?"

"I am as her next of kin."

"Is that why you're buying art from Rowan? To add to the gallery?"

"You should be out hunting down my wife's murderer not harassing me about my art purchases." Doring waved his hand toward the door and splashed his drink on his hand and cuff.

Good. His question flustered the man. He'd bet his collection of old T.V. shows that Doring had a part in his wife's death. He may not have driven the spear into her chest, but he paid the man who did.

## Chapter Twenty-eight

Shandra drove home, grumbling about men. Ryan hadn't wanted her to be there while he questioned Sidney. But tossing her out after the man threw his tantrum, irked. There was a reason Sidney didn't want her there. She made him angry just like his wife.

Sheba whined from the back seat when they turned up the driveway.

"Yeah, me too. I'm happy to be home." Shandra patted the big head that nudged her shoulder. "I wish Ella would stop putting dreams in my head and let me get back to my peaceful life."

She parked the Jeep and headed to the studio intent on working on the souvenir pieces. Her inventory was low and there were still two more months of summer tourists headed to Huckleberry.

Dipping the coasters in glaze didn't require a lot of thought. Her mind wandered to Oscar Rowan. Very little was known about the artist. The only work of his on his website were pieces that showed an artist still looking for his style or an artist who was inconsistent. Not good traits for someone wanting to make a living off their work. Artistry and emotion twined as one in the warrior statue. The diversity on his site didn't show the same connection.

Placing the lid on the bucket of glaze, she washed her hands and headed to the house. Once she sat in front of the computer with a cup of tea, she started googling bronze warrior statues. Two hours later she had printed pages that proved Oscar Rowan did not sculpt the warrior statue. It was part of a collection made by a western artist who had passed away ten years earlier. Only collectors of western art would know the artist name on the statue was forged.

Paula had to know the statue was worth far more than the price set on it. She had to have done the research and discovered it wasn't an original of Oscar Rowan. "Was that why he killed you?"

Shandra dialed Ryan, but his phone went straight to voice mail. She left a message that she had incriminating evidence against Oscar Rowan. Her stomach growled, and she wandered into the kitchen to make a salad for dinner.

After she'd eaten, she paced the living room. When would Ryan call? She had patience when it came to molding clay or being part of a creative process, but in everything else, she lacked her grandmother's easy-going tolerance to wait out life's hiccups.

If she could get photos of the statue and find a foundry stamp or date on the statue or base, she could further incriminate the imposter artist. But how was she to get into the gallery? Ryan took away Naomi's key. Juan was locked up.

"Why aren't you calling me back?" She peered at Ryan's name on her phone.

The phone rang. She tossed it up before juggling it into her hands. "I'm glad you—"

"Ms. Higheagle, this is Liz Perry with the DEA. We're allowing the artists with work in the Doring Gallery to pick up their pieces tonight. After tonight the building will be locked up, and you'll have to go through the local authorities to gain custody of your property."

The business-like, bored tone didn't set off any alarms. "I can be there in an hour."

"Come in the back door. We don't want civilians thinking the gallery is open for business." Agent Perry hung up.

Shandra collected her thoughts. She'd not heard of Agent Liz Perry, but the voice souned a bit like the no-nonsense woman who'd stopped her from walking through the alley when the DEA were taking the evidence from the back of Doring Gallery. The vase was a fifteen-hundred-dollar piece. It wouldn't be practical to have it tied up in a bureaucratic nightmare.

She grabbed a sweatshirt off the coat tree, picked up her purse, and headed to the barn.

Strains of an old western tune floated from inside. Her eyes adjusted to the dark interior, and she spotted Lil cleaning Oliver's stall. The old gelding had been Shandra's horse at the ranch in Montana. He was the only thing she'd brought with her of her childhood.

Shandra walked over and scratched the sorrel between the ears. "I'm headed back to town. A DEA agent called and said if I want the vase that was in the Doring Gallery I need to pick it up tonight before it gets caught up in legalities."

Lil stopped scooping and leaned on the manure fork. "You sure that's a good idea? Seems strange they'd call you there in the middle of the night."

Shandra faced Lil. "They have probably discovered the same thing I did about Oscar Rowan. I bet he was tied up with the drugs and killed Paula. I'm sure they want to get this all wrapped up and move on."

Lil shook her head. "I don't like it. You call that detective?"

"I left a message telling him about Oscar. When he calls me back, I'll tell him where I am." Shandra gave Oliver one last scratch before walking out of the barn. All her bases were covered between telling Lil and leaving the message for Ryan.

~*~

Ryan sat in Ruthie's Diner waiting for Oscar Rowan to show. He'd discovered from a conversation with Ruthie that the man came in for dinner every night at seven. Since he'd been unable to locate where the man was staying, this seemed like the best way to confront him about his visit to Doring earlier.

He patted his empty phone holster and grimaced. His phone went dead while he was on the computer trying to discover Rowan's whereabouts. The phone was in his vehicle charging. He felt as naked and vulnerable without his phone as he did without his gun.

Baylor entered the diner. He scanned the booths. His brow started to furrow then smoothed out when he spotted Ryan. He nodded then sat at the end of the counter farthest from him. Ryan peeked at his watch.

Five till seven.

He took a sip of his coffee and watched Baylor over the rim. The man was anxious about something. His left leg bounced and his fingers drummed on the counter. The waitress placed a glass of soda in front of him.

"You want the usual?" she asked.

Baylor leaned toward her, and Ryan couldn't hear what he said. She smiled and wrote on her pad before disappearing into the kitchen.

Rowan entered and started toward Baylor. The DEA agent barely shook his head. Rowan changed direction, plopping down in a booth behind him.

It appeared Baylor and Rowan used the café as a rendezvous spot. Ryan picked up his coffee cup and sauntered over to the booth. He dropped into the seat opposite Rowan.

"You're a hard man to track down."

"Didn't know anyone was looking for me." Rowan shot a brief glance toward Baylor then slouched into the seat.

He tried to appear relaxed and unconcerned, but his left eyebrow twitched and the floor under Ryan's food vibrated from Rowan's toe tapping.

"What did you and Sidney Doring have to talk about this afternoon?"

"He's buying one of my statues."

There had been enough time since Ryan's visit with Doring, he could have contacted Rowan and told him what to say. "That why he gave you an envelope of money?"

Rowan's eyes widened, then narrowed, and he glared. "How did you know he gave me money?"

"Good guess." Ryan smiled. He loved it when the bad guys slipped up. "Was he really paying you for a statue or was he paying you to kill his wife?"

Rowan's gaze shot to Baylor, who stood up, dropped money on the counter, and left the diner.

"I don't know what you two have going on, but he isn't going to get you out of a murder charge." Ryan slid to the end of the booth to stand.

Rowan grabbed his arm stopping him. "I didn't kill anyone. And I'm not going to let you or Baylor pin it on me."

Ryan slid back into the seat. "Tell me your story. I'll decide if I take you in or not."

Rowan licked his lips and scanned the diner. "I'm an informant for the DEA. They've been curious about Paula Doring for some time and set me up as an artist to get into her graces. She tended to be very friendly with the male artists. If you know what I mean."

Ryan nodded.

"I figured out she was a drop-off for goods moving through the Rafael chain. I'd been playing up to her to get in and learn where they went next, but then I saw the photos of Joyce in her drawer and when I heard Joyce had overdosed, I discovered a whole new side to Paula. I've been giving information about her drug dealings to Baylor and information about her clandestine meetings and hatred of Joyce to Doring." He raised his hands. "That's all, just selling information to whoever wanted it. I don't kill people."

"Not with your hands maybe, but the information you gave Doring may have killed his wife." Ryan tossed a five on the table for his coffee and hurried out to his vehicle.

He'd missed two calls. The first one from Shandra. He smiled. She'd figured out Rowan wasn't who he pretended to be. The second number he didn't know, and they didn't leave a message. He hit the phone icon and waited.

"Hello?" The voice sounded like an older female.

"This is Detective Greer. Who is this and why did you call?"

"This is Lil, Shandra's helper. Detective you need to get to the Doring Gallery. A DEA agent called and told Shandra she had to pick up her vase tonight. She could be in trouble."

Ryan pushed the phone off button and cranked his car's ignition. He didn't trust Baylor. But if he'd call, surely Shandra would have called me. Was there more than one corrupt DEA agent?

Chapter Twenty-nine

Shandra parked in the alley. The vase was one of her larger ones and she didn't want to pack it any farther than she had to. Where were the other artists' cars? And what about the artists who weren't local? How long would they have to wait to get their pieces?

The door was unlocked and standing open with light spilling out into the back alley. She stepped inside and stopped, staring at the empty room. The only thing left was the table and a workbench along one wall. Every scrap of paper or packing was gone. She made a note to drop a hint about possible drugs in her studio to the DEA the next time she needed it cleaned.

A light flickered in the gallery. She walked toward it. "Hello? Agent Perry? It's Shandra, Shandra Higheagle." Her voice echoed through the high ceilings. A shiver slithered up her arms and settled as a hard cold knot in the middle of her chest.

"Agent Perry?" Her feet continued one in front of the other carrying her into the gallery. The only lights were slender beams leaking out around the office door. She glanced back at the well-lit back room. "Why aren't the lights on? How can we find our work?"

No answer. The knot in her chest grew tighter. She stopped at the door to the office. Her hand reached out to grasp the doorknob. If she locked herself in the office, she could use the phone to call Ryan. The realization this appeared to be a set-up shifted her fear to anger. She'd blindly walked into this because she was sure her findings had discovered the murderer. But Ryan had suspicions about Rowan and Baylor.

Shandra opened the office door and shut it, then hurried as quietly as she could back down the wall to a dark shadow. She'd wait for whoever had lured her here to go in the office after her, and then she'd run for the back door.

She didn't have a clue where her adversary hid.

Air wafted and the soft sound of steps came toward her from the gallery. She peered into the darkness. An image emerged when someone walked into an open section that had the faint street light glow. The silhouette wasn't of a woman.

What was he doing here? Her heart thudded in her chest and echoed in her ears like the ceremonial drums. Why hadn't he answered her when she called out?

Her adversary flung open the office door. Before the door knob hitting the wall echoed, she ran for the back door. Her hands hit the now-closed back door. When had the door closed? Her palms stung from the impact. She rattled the knob.

*Locked!*

There was no place to hide in the empty room.
She spun around and faced her assailant.

Baylor.

He swaggered toward her, a smirk on his lips. His
gaze bore into her.

"Why are you holding me here? How did you get
Agent Perry to call me?" She pressed her back against
the door. Her only chance now was to get to the front of
the gallery and break a glass window or cause some
kind of ruckus to get the attention of someone out for
an evening stroll.

"I've never met such a nosy artist before. Agent
Perry does what I tell her to do. It's amazing what you
can get career-minded underlings to do." Baylor stalked
toward her. He didn't have any weapons in his hands.

But he's an agent. He could probably kill me with
his bare hands.

"Do my questions bother you? They shouldn't if
you didn't kill anyone." She edged along the wall,
hoping to race past him.

She pumped her arm back getting ready to sprint.

He lunged at her, grasping her arm tight.

"No, you aren't getting away. You have a letter to
write." Baylor hauled her, dragging her heels, to the
office.

"I don't feel like writing a letter," she remarked as
he shoved her into the desk chair.

"I don't care how you feel. Once you write the
letter you aren't going to feel anything again."

Frantic to find a weapon, Shandra searched the
office and noticed a coil of rope by the door. Is he going
to tie me up?

"Pick up the pen." He pointed to a pen sitting next

to a blank piece of paper. "Now write: I can't live with myself anymore. I killed Paula. And sign your name."

Shandra shook her head. "No one would believe that. Why would I kill Paula? I barely knew the woman."

"I'll spread the word you were wanting to take over her drug route."

A laugh burst out of her before she could stop it. "Why?"

"It doesn't matter why. I'm a DEA agent and people will believe me." He grabbed the back of her neck and squeezed. "Write."

His fingers dug into her neck muscle, making her left arm go numb. She placed the pen on the paper and tried to concentrate on writing what he'd dictated. Her mind flashed to the brief moments she'd connected with Ryan. She wanted more of those. If she didn't find a way to get out of this room, she'd never have a chance to see where their relationship could go.

"Please, I can't feel my fingers to write."

He eased up but kept his hand on her neck. If he was trying to intimidate her it was working.

"I gather from this note you're having me write, you plan to kill me and make it look like a suicide." This is where her grandmother's stories of how her people found courage and pride in dying for their principles came in handy. She knew no one, especially Ryan, would believe she killed Paula. Ryan would seek out this man and bring him to trial.

His fingers tightened on her neck again. "Your remorse got the better of you."

"What about you? Do you have any remorse about killing Paula?" She wasn't sure he had, but that had to be the reason he was making her the patsy.

"She was going to tell the Rafaels that I was an agent. I couldn't have her blow my cover. Not after I'd withheld evidence from her husband and killed the only person who could have spilled everything."

"You have two murders on your hands? Who did you kill besides Paula?" she asked nonchalantly, but inside fear bounced around like a prickly pear.

He glared at her.

"What's it matter? You're going to kill me anyway. At least let me die having my questions answered."

~*~

Ryan spotted Shandra's Jeep. He pulled up alongside and exited his vehicle with his gun drawn. The gallery door was locked. Thankful he hadn't turned in all the keys to the building, he slid his copy slowly into the lock and just as cautiously turned the knob and eased the door open a crack. Light seeped out around the door.

He took a deep breath, plastered his body against the side of the building, and flung the door open.

Nothing.

No sound.

He poked the nose of his Glock into the opening. Nothing.

A quick glance showed an empty room. With caution, he entered the building and crept to the doorway that entered the gallery. Light shone under the office door. Were Shandra and Baylor in the office? Using the slim line of light as a beacon, he proceeded forward. The muffled sound of voices caught his attention.

Ryan leaned against the outside wall of the office

and pressed his ear to the wall.

"So who did you kill besides Paula? Another informant?"

Shandra's steady voice eased the fear he'd had for her safety, but her question baffled him.

"Not an informant. Someone who knew my informant before he turned narc. Paula, Joyce, and my informant all hung out in the same crowds in Seattle."

Rage started at Ryan's toes and flamed up to his face. Baylor! He knew there was something not right with the guy even if he did come highly recommended by the State Police Captain.

"You killed Joyce?" Shandra's voice held less bravado.

"I wasn't going to let some druggie ruin what I'd worked years to establish. Do you know how hard it is to get in with a Mexican cartel? To get them to confide in anyone other than their 'family'?" The man took a deep breath. "I'd worked years cultivating Rowan to move into the cartel, I did everything but kiss Paula's ass to get her to help plant Rowan. When she recognized Joyce as Dale Young's girlfriend I had to get her out of the picture before he showed up."

"He who? Rowan or Dale?" Shandra asked the same question Ryan was wondering.

"Both. Dale Young agreed to go under for us if we gave him a lighter sentence and changed his name and appearance." Baylor snarled. "But he made a lousy informant. He couldn't hide some of his tics. It would have only been a matter of time and Joyce would have figured it out. Then Paula got greedy. She wanted money for her silence in not only my identity but my part in Joyce's overdose."

Ryan heard enough. He kicked open the door. "Police! Get your hands up!"

Baylor hauled Shandra up in front of him. He didn't have a weapon in his hands.

Ryan flicked a glance at Shandra.

She dropped her gaze to the floor, and then stared straight in his eyes. She would drop when he gave the signal.

*May the blessings of Saint Patrick be with me.* He nodded.

Shandra slipped out of Baylor's arm and dropped to the floor.

Ryan pulled the trigger.

Shandra hit the floor and started scrambling on her hands and knees toward Ryan. She didn't stop until she'd climbed his body and he'd wrapped his arm around her. Her body shook from the terror and the adrenaline racing through her veins.

"Are you okay?" Ryan's voice penetrated the ringing in her ears.

She nodded and caught an acrid whiff of gun powder. "Is he?"

"I need you to sit down while I cuff him." Ryan held a gun on the man as he got her seated in the chair by the door and rolled the moaning Baylor over to cuff his arms behind his back.

Shandra stared at the back of the man who saved her life. She'd hoped someone would arrive and save her from Baylor's hands. That it had been Ryan… She looked up. *Ella, did you have something to do with this?*

Ryan called on the phone for a car to come pick up Baylor. He came back over and crouched in front of the chair. "Why did you come here all by yourself?"

She shook her head. "I'd determined Rowan/Dale Young had murdered Paula. When a female DEA agent called and said I could pick up my vase, I thought she was legitimate." She frowned. "I don't understand why she didn't get curious about his order."

"I'll not only ask Baylor that but the woman agent as well. I heard his confessions to you about Joyce and Paula. I can't believe he would stoop that far to maintain his cover." Ryan peered over his shoulder at Baylor. His attention returned to her. "I want you to drive straight home. Don't come down off your mountain for anyone or anything. I'll come up in the morning and get your statement."

She stared into his eyes and nodded. After tonight, she might not come down off her mountain for months.

Chapter Thirty

Shandra was showered and dressed and in the middle of making a batch of waffles when Ryan drove up. She answered the door and smiled watching Ryan wrestle with Sheba and scratch her floppy ears.

"Just in time for breakfast. Come on in." She left the door open and headed to the kitchen. The sound of boot heels following her through the house made her smile.

"It smells great." Ryan helped himself to a cup of coffee and sat at the bar watching her pour batter into the waffle maker. He had dark circles under his eyes.

"Did you get much sleep last night?"

"Only about two hours. Once I'd questioned Baylor and Agent Perry, booked Baylor, and filed all the paperwork it was four."

She placed a hand on his freshly-shaved cheek. He'd taken the time to shave, shower, and look as handsome as the first day she laid eyes on him. He smelled woodsy and clean. "I'm sorry. Did you learn how he rationalized calling me to the gallery to Agent Perry?"

"He told Perry he thought you were the killer, and that I was too attracted to you to see it. He wanted to get you alone to get to the truth." Ryan's brow furrowed, and his mouth formed a straight line of disapproval.

"After you left the gallery and I emerged with Baylor in handcuffs, Agent Perry stepped out of the shadows and tried to take him away from me. She figured he was up to something and had been staking the building out. When I refused to give him to her, she followed me to the police station and added some more information that will keep Baylor behind bars for a long time."

Ryan gazed into her eyes. "He was right about one thing."

Her face heated. "What?"

"I am attracted to you." He grasped one of her hands and held it. "The sheriff gave me four days off for all the work I've done. I was thinking about hanging around Huckleberry and doing some hiking."

Bubbles of happiness tickled her belly. "You know how to ride a horse, sheep rancher?"

"I've been on one a time or two."

"After breakfast, I'd like to show you my mountain."

"That's the kind of R and R I need after the fright you gave me last night."

He tugged her hand, drawing her around the counter to him. Shandra went, knowing he would kiss her. After all, this scene had played over and over in her dream last night. And Ella had been smiling.

Book Two in the Shandra Higheagle Mystery series:

## Tarnished Remains
By
Paty Jager

Chapter One

Shandra Higheagle leaned on the shovel handle, staring into the pine forest to her right. She loved her excursions up Huckleberry Mountain to collect clay. She'd purchased this land two years ago for this pocket of clay. The yellowish mud, when cleaned and purified, enhanced her art. Using Mother Nature's bounty to make her inspirations come to life enriched the overall appearance and authenticity of her work. That she used natural clay and formed pottery as her ancestors once had, made her pieces unique and sought after.

Enough musing and wasting time. She raised the shovel, sunk the metal blade into the ground six inches, and pulled out a shovel full of yellow clay. The packed soil held enough moisture to cling to the shovel. She knocked the blade against the top of the bucket, dropping the clay in. A good shove with her foot set the spade into the ground for another scoop. The metal grated on something hard. Possibly a rock. She'd hit a few while digging clay in this pocket.

Wiggling the shovel, she shoved again and pulled up another chunk of clay. Her artistic imagination saw a chunk on the side that resembled the shape of a cowboy boot heel. Shandra chuckled at her imagination and knocked the shovel against her plastic bucket. The chunk broke apart and a boot heel fell to the outside of the bucket.

Shandra eased down onto her knees beside the bucket. Using her trowel, she broke up the rest of the chunk. Nothing.

Perhaps someone, years ago, while riding or hiking up here lost a boot heel.

She stood, picked up the shovel, and sunk the blade into the ground not far from the last scoop.

Instead of the usual high pitched zing of the metal slicing through the soil there was the sound of a stick breaking. She shoved the blade farther with her booted foot. Another crunch, and she shoved down on the handle, freeing a section of clay larger than her usual scoopful.

Tingles raced up her spine at the sight of something white sticking out of the clay. She lifted and tipped the shovel, dumping the clod on the ground.

Her dead Nez Perce grandmother's face flashed through her mind.

"Ella, what have I stumbled onto?" Shandra asked her grandmother.

She picked up her trowel and knelt beside the chunk of clay. Slow, small cuts with the trowel soon revealed she'd dug up a leather cowboy boot with intricate detailing and the foot it encased.

She'd made a thorough search of all the Native American burial grounds before purchasing this ranch and mountain. There wasn't an Indian burial ground on the premise. She'd made certain. That information, and seeing the detail on the boot, she was pretty sure this wasn't an Indian.

Reaching into her back pocket, Shandra slid her cell phone out. One faint bar of coverage up here.

Nine-one-one or Detective Ryan Greer?

Admitting to herself she wouldn't mind seeing the detective again, she punched in his number. They'd met a month ago when she'd been a suspect in a gallery owner's murder. They'd come away from the event friends. She also wasn't shy to admit, she'd like to become more than friends with the handsome detective. They'd spent several days after his last case in Huckleberry talking, riding horses, and getting to know more about one another. She hadn't heard from him in a couple of weeks.

"Detective Greer."

"Ryan, it's Shandra Higheagle—"

"Shandra, I've been meaning to call you. Work has been dragging me out in the early hours and dropping me into bed close to midnight."

She smiled at his boyish need to explain why he hadn't called. "I'm afraid I'm going to add to your work."

"Don't tell me you found another dead body," he said in a joking tone.

"I'm afraid I did."

"Where? Are you in danger?" His demeanor went from joking to all business.

The sound of tires dragging against gravel proved he was out in his SUV somewhere in Weippe County.

"I'm on my property digging clay. No, I'm not in danger. This person looks to have been here a while." She gave him all the details.

"I'll be there in an hour. Don't do any more digging."

His siren shrilled in the background.

"Go to the ranch and have Lil bring you up."

"Will do."

Shandra closed her phone and stared down at the bone and the leather boot. "Who are you and why are you on this mountain?"

Even though Ryan told her not to dig any more, her curiosity got the better of her. At least she'd read enough about archeology digs for Native American remains and artifacts that she knew to use her hands and go slow to not damage any evidence.

In the time it would take Ryan to get here, she could have something more than a foot and boot for him to investigate.

~*~

Ryan pulled into Shandra's ranch, his siren still shrieking and lights flashing. The serene cabin and studio in the middle of the forest made him feel like an interloper. He switched off the lights and siren immediately, and then the engine.

Crazy Lil, Shandra's hired hand, approached the car with a scowl. "What you scarin' all the animals for?"

Ryan stepped out of the vehicle. Crazy Lil's head came to the middle of his chest. For a small woman she gave off a larger presence. He knew little about the woman other than she worked for Shandra Higheagle and all the locals called her Crazy Lil, but not her employer.

He'd met Shandra under the worst of circumstances a month ago when an overzealous newbie tried to arrest her for murder when she was found in the same room as a recently murdered gallery owner.

His heart picked up pace remembering his first encounter with the intriguing woman and the days they spent together after he solved her case.

"Wanna wipe that grin off your lips and tell me why you came screaming in here?" Crazy Lil smacked him in his solar plexus, causing air to whoosh between his teeth and lips.

"There's no need to hit an officer of the law," he snapped, rubbing his chest. "Shandra called. Said she found a body and wanted me to come check it out."

The woman's face paled. "A body?"

"Yes. She said to have you bring me. She found it where she collects clay." Ryan waved to the passenger side of his SUV. "Hop in."

Crazy Lil shook her head. "Can't get there with a vehicle. Have to ride a horse."

"How does Shandra bring down the clay?" He knew the woman was tenacious, but he couldn't see her packing buckets of clay off the mountain.

"She's got horses." Crazy Lil turned toward the barn and corrals. "You can ride Oliver." She whistled.

One horse trotted to the corral railing and hung his head over. He had some age on him judging from the gray in his red coat and a good sway to his back. Ryan might have worked in the big city of Chicago, but he grew up on a ranch forty miles from this mountain. He knew horses, and he knew how to ride.

"I don't think that sorrel will make it up the mountain without someone on his back. Let alone carrying me." He waited for a response from the woman.

She spun about. "You gonna talk or you gonna help

me saddle up the horses?"

Ryan studied the woman marching into the barn. She was either an ornery, abrupt, no-nonsense person or socially inept. Given what Shandra had said about the woman rarely leaving the ranch and growing up here, he'd go with socially inept.

He hustled into the barn behind the woman and was relieved to see two younger, spryer geldings in stalls. One was the horse he rode when Shandra gave him a tour of her property.

"Do I get Duke? He and I got along fine the last time I rode him." He walked to the stall with the bay horse, hanging a wide, white-blazed face over the gate.

"You might as well, you aren't riding my horse." Crazy Lil pointed to a saddle hanging over a stand. "Use that one."

Ryan picked up the halter hanging by Duke's stall and opened the gate. "Hey boy, remember me?"

Fifteen minutes later, Ryan had Duke tacked up and his gear stowed on the saddle. He threw a leg over his mount and followed Crazy Lil up the side of the mountain. This was his first trek into the mountains for a body. He hoped whatever Shandra stumble into didn't get her caught up in trouble. The woman seemed to be a magnet for murder.

## About the Author

Award winning author Paty Jager ranches with her husband of thirty-five years. They've raised hay, hogs, cattle, kids, and grandkids. Her first book was published in 2006 and since then she has published seventeen books, five novellas, and two anthologies in the western romance and action adventure genres. She enjoys riding horses, playing with her grandkids, judging 4-H contests and fairs, and outdoor activities. To learn more about her books and her life, or to click on links to take you to the ebook sales sites, you can visit her website.

**http://www.patyjager.net**

**Other Shandra Higheagle Mysteries coming soon:**

*Tarnished Remains* - February 2015

*Deadly Aim* - March 2015

Thank you for purchasing this Windtree Press
publication. For other books of the heart, please visit
our website at www.windtreepress.com.

For questions or more information contact us at
info@windtreepress.com.

Windtree Press
www.windtreepress.com